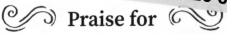

Praise for

ME, MY DAD AND THE
END OF THE RAINBOW

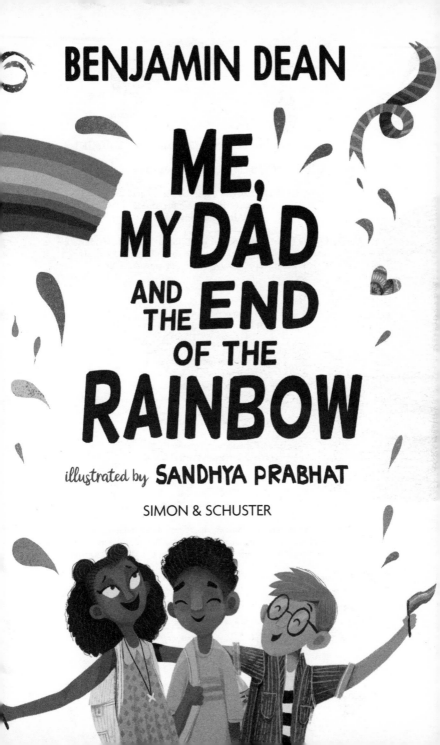

BENJAMIN DEAN

ME, MY DAD AND THE END OF THE RAINBOW

illustrated by **SANDHYA PRABHAT**

SIMON & SCHUSTER

First published in Great Britain in 2021 by Simon & Schuster UK Ltd

1 3 5 7 9 10 8 6 4 2

Simon & Schuster UK Ltd
1st Floor, 222 Gray's Inn Road
London WC1X 8HB

www.simonandschuster.co.uk
www.simonandschuster.com.au
www.simonandschuster.co.in

Simon & Schuster Australia, Sydney
Simon & Schuster India, New Delhi

A CIP catalogue record for this book
is available from the British Library.

PB ISBN 978-1-4711-9973-8
eBook ISBN 978-1-4711-9974-5
Audio ISBN 978-1-4711-9986-8

Printed and bound by CPI Group (UK) Ltd, Croydon, CR0 4YY

To Mum, for everything,
and to my best friends, for being family.

CHAPTER 1

SOME SECRETS TO TELL

So, you're standing in the bookshop reading this, right? Or maybe you've just unwrapped this book for your birthday in front of all of your friends and you've quickly flicked to the first page to see what kind of story you're in for. Well, can you do me a favour before we get started? I need you to look over your shoulder. Your right shoulder or your left shoulder, it doesn't really matter which one. But I need you to look over one of them and double-check that nobody is behind you. If there's one thing I know about people, it's that they are all very curious, and by that, I mean they don't know how to mind their own business.

Okay, so the coast is clear? Good, because I'm about to tell you some of my most secret secrets and I don't want just anybody reading them. But, before I tell you my secrets, you have to PROMISE not to tell anybody else. Not one single soul. I mean it! This has to stay between us, okay? Also, it's probably best that your parents don't know you're reading this book. I don't want them to think that I'm giving you any bad ideas. This book is a little adventure, sure, but I don't want you getting in trouble.

I'm Archie by the way. Archie Albright. I would tell you my middle name but I'm not sure I trust you *that* much just yet. Maybe later.

Right, so the first secret. I'm actually four feet seven inches tall. Yes, I told Amber Patel that I was four feet nine inches tall and yes that was a lie. But I didn't think she would be my friend if I said I was four feet seven inches tall because Caveman Kyle is exactly five feet tall and everybody wants to be his friend. To be honest, I'm not quite sure why the first thing I ever said to Amber Patel was 'Hi, I'm four feet nine inches tall' but I can't take it back now.

Fortunately, my two best friends in the world, Seb and Bell, know my true height and don't hold it against me. In fact, they know all my secrets, even the ones I can barely admit to myself. The three of us have been best friends for a year now, since Bell joined our school from one 'up North' as Dad puts it. Before she came to Vale Gate High, it was just me and Seb, blundering through life together. I'm glad there's three of us now.

The second secret is pretty much why I'm telling you all of this in the first place. It's important to the story but it makes me cringe to think about, even now. You see, my mum and dad kind of hate each other. They try to pretend that they don't when I'm in the room, but they're not very good at hiding it. Adults love to think that us kids are dumb, but half the time we know way more than they give us credit for.

Mum and Dad haven't always hated each other. In fact, they used to be in love, not that you would know it now. According to my gran, they met on Dad's twenty-first birthday, when Dad still had a giant afro that he cared for more than anything in the world. When he tried to say hello, he tripped over and poured his drink, which was blood red, down Mum's dress, which was white and brand new. If you ask me, that sounds exactly like something Dad would do. He can be really clumsy.

Mum is a foot or so shorter than Dad, even when she's up on her tiptoes. But in all the photos they've collected over the years, she looks even smaller thanks to Dad's afro.

Back then, Mum wore clothes that made her shoulders look bigger than they were, and her hair was blown out into these dark brown curls that fell all around her face, framing it like a picture. Now, it's always tied back because Mum thinks it just gets in her way otherwise.

While Mum still looks something like the pictures she has saved in the family photo albums, Dad couldn't look more different. He shaved off his hair the same year I was born. He used to say that it fell out from the stress, a joke that made Mum laugh no matter how many times he told it. He wears glasses now too, although only when he reads and not all the time like he should, which Mum nags him about because his eyesight will only get worse. She used to nag him about it, anyway. She doesn't so much any more.

Anyway, they were in love and now they're not. Even though Dad moved out and they rarely talk unless it's about me, Gran says they still love each other deep, deep down and I think that's true. I'm still getting used to this weird new normal, even if it sometimes feels like a storm cloud is floating over my head. I see Dad all the time for our weekly arcade trips and video game nights, but it still makes my heart jump when he drops me off at home and drives away to his new house.

The final secret I have to tell you is something really important, so I hope I can trust you to keep it to yourself.

What happened next, it was all my fault.

Sure, Seb and Bell had their say in the matter, but the whole idea was mine and I dragged them into it. They just came along because they're my best friends and that's what best friends do. It wasn't even Oscar's or Dean's fault, though Mum and Dad would disagree on that specific point. If I have one criticism of them both, it's that they really should have been paying more attention. But I guess I dragged them into this whole mess too. So yeah, I take the blame for everything. Well, almost everything. I just needed to get that off my chest.

You're probably wondering what I'm talking about and, to be honest, I'm not sure if I'm even telling this story very well. So I think I'd better go back to the point where this all started, because that seems like the obvious place to begin a story. It was the middle of the night – no really, it was, I'm not just saying that for dramatic effect – and it suddenly hit me that things were starting to get a little weird.

CHAPTER 2

AN AWKWARD BEGINNING

I knew there was something wrong. Don't ask me how I knew there was something wrong, I just had this feeling. It was almost as if the Earth had tilted just a little, but I was the only one who could feel it and therefore I was the only one who knew for a fact that something was definitely, without a doubt, one-hundred-per-cent wrong.

It all started with a phone call earlier that day. I never usually answer the phone if I can help it, but Mum and Dad were across the street at the Bakers' house, which was odd in itself. I'd watched from the window, my tummy a knot of nerves, as they walked over the road, at least a metre of space between them. I hadn't seen them that close together in a while. Mr Baker, who is actually called

Richard, is Dad's friend, and Mrs Baker, who is actually called Annette, is Mum's friend. I don't go to the Bakers' house because I think it's boring. However, I was curious when Dad arrived at the house unannounced and Mum grabbed her coat, giving me a peck on the forehead at the door. Apparently, the trip to the Bakers' house was for adults only, which meant I couldn't go with them. This only made my curiosity boil even more.

So, the phone started to ring and I ignored it at first because talking on the phone is awkward and embarrassing and usually never good news. But it started to ring again so I had no choice. I picked it up and held it gingerly to my ear, hoping it would just be a wrong number and I could go back to playing video games. But it wasn't a wrong number. It was Doctor Sammy.

Doctor Sammy's real name is actually Doctor Ferguson. She doesn't like that name, though, and insists we call her Sammy. She's not a *doctor* doctor, like the ones you go to see if you're ill. If I'm not well, Mum or Dad take me to see Doctor Kiligrew. But if we go to see Doctor Sammy, then something entirely different is wrong.

The first time I went to see Doctor Sammy, I was only

little. Mum and Dad took me because, when I was four years old, I hadn't started speaking yet and everybody was pretty worried about me. I don't remember what that was like because I was four and nobody remembers that far back. I'm twelve now and, if you hadn't already guessed, I talk way too much.

The last time we went to see Doctor Sammy was just before Dad decided to move out. Mum and Dad had been arguing for a while. It was always about nothing in particular, but it was never-ending. So they went to Doctor Sammy's office together in a bid to make things better. But they couldn't even agree on that and, after less than a month, they stopped going altogether and told me they were getting a divorce instead, which just started yet another argument. The only thing they seemed to agree on was that they both wanted me to see Doctor Sammy too. So they took me to her office. Doctor Sammy insisted that neither of them sat in on the conversation. It was just me and her talking over a ginormous desk about everything that was happening. It was weird and awkward and included a lot of questions like 'and how do you feel about that?' but it made Mum and Dad happy – or happier – that I was going.

Anyway, that was almost three months ago, so I was more than a little confused when I picked up the phone and heard Doctor Sammy's voice.

'Hi, Archie, it's Doctor Sammy.'

'Hello,' I mumbled. Like I said, I hate talking on the phone.

'Is your dad there?'

'No, he's across the street at the Bakers' house.'

'Ah, I see. Is your mum there instead?'

I shook my head, then remembered that Doctor Sammy couldn't see that.

'No, she's with Dad and he's across the street at the Bakers' house.'

'Okay, no problem. Could you get your dad to give me a call back when he's home?'

'Uh-huh.'

'No rush, just whenever he's back.'

'Okay.'

Doctor Sammy said goodbye and hung up the phone. I frowned but didn't really think anything of it again until Mum and Dad got home a little while later.

'Doctor Sammy called,' I said offhandedly as I marched into the kitchen in search of snacks. I had ducked my head into the crisp cupboard, trying to sneak a second packet under my shirt, so it wasn't until I turned around that I realized everybody was frozen to the spot. Dad, in particular, looked as if he were about to throw up. Mum was beginning to blush, breathing heavily.

'What did she say?' Dad said, turning greener by the second.

'She just asked you to call her back.' I looked from Mum to Dad. They were sharing a look between themselves.

'Okay, sweetheart. Nothing to worry about!' Mum patted me on the head – she does that a lot – and steered me out of the room. Just as we were leaving the kitchen, I saw Dad pick up the phone. But before I could see anything else, he closed the door behind him, which I think meant he didn't want to be heard.

I ducked into the living room to wait for Dad because he'd promised we could play *Mario Kart* before he went home. That was our thing and I didn't see why a phone call with Doctor Sammy had to ruin it. But even from the living room, I could hear Mum muttering to herself as she mounted the stairs.

'Running up my phone bill and he doesn't even live here any more,' she said, without caring who could hear

her. She closed her bedroom door with a little more force than necessary.

When Dad finally got off the phone and came into the living room, he looked ... well, a little odd, like he might be in a daze or hypnotized by something I couldn't see. He fell down onto the sofa in a slump, stroking his stubble absently. His eyes, a brown so dark that they were almost black, stared intently at the wall, looking through it rather than at anything in particular. But he snapped out of it when I offered him a controller, grinning mischievously and holding it aloft.

'You're going down, kid,' he said, his voice deep and booming like some of our favourite movie villains. We traded trash-talk until the game finally booted to life, offering nothing but silence while we took on the important task of picking a character that would race us to victory.

'How's that smoke looking?' Dad grinned, shooting out into the lead as the race started. 'Think you can keep up?'

I ignored his gloating, leaning with my controller like I was really driving the car on screen, Baby Mario leaning with me until I was finally in second place, right behind Dad's Bowser.

'You were saying?' I smirked as I drifted around a corner and slipped into the lead with one lap to go.

The race was tight until, at the very last moment, I slipped on a banana peel I'd thrown down the lap before. My car spun off the track for just a second, but it was enough for Dad to swoop in and cross the line in first place.

'Winner!' he hollered, jubilant and smug. 'There's just no beating the best, Arch. Valiant battle, though, I'll give you that. You'll make a fine driver someday. Just look out for any banana peels lying about.'

Dropping the controller at my feet, I leaped into action, barrelling into Dad so he fell off the sofa and landed with a soft thud on the carpet. I sat on his back and waved my hands in the air, counting to three. Dad laughed and pretended to struggle, but he let me get the win and eventually tapped out. We fell back onto the sofa in fits of giggles, exhausted. Just another casual night in the Albright household.

After that, we watched a movie – Dad, as the winner, chose *Top Gun*, like I knew he would – until it was finally time for him to go home. In the Before Days, Mum would've laid out a feast of snacks and cuddled up between us, only to complain about our choice of film and eventually fall asleep on Dad's shoulder. Sometimes they'd both doze off, gently snoring in time with each other. There was no chance of that now.

From the top of the stairs, I snapped to attention and gave Dad an over-the-top salute as he plucked his coat off the hook. 'Goodbye, Father, sergeant of House Albright and runner up of phone bills,' I said in the most dramatic voice I could muster. Dad snapped to attention too, returning my salute.

'I bid thee a good evening and goodnight,' he mimicked. Just as he turned to leave, he seemed to think of something. 'Runner up of phone bills?'

I shot a pointed look at Mum's closed bedroom door.

'Ah, of course.' Dad smiled to himself. 'Well, she's called me a lot worse, I guess. Still on for Friday night?'

I nodded. We were tied three-all on the air-hockey table at Mack's Arcade. Me and Dad had been going there every Friday for as long as I could remember. Mum was always happy to get us out of the house for a couple of hours so she could curl up on the sofa and share a scandal or two with her friends over the phone.

'Be prepared to lose. I've been practising,' I said, puffing out my chest.

'Fighting talk, young sir.' Dad nodded at the bedroom door. 'Make sure she's okay, will you?'

'Sure,' I said, shrinking into myself slightly at the thought that she might not be.

And that was it. Dad left, Mum reappeared, and I got into bed wondering what on Earth that phone call could've been about. That's why I was awake in the middle of the night, thinking about what Doctor Sammy could possibly want with Dad now. Yes, something was definitely wrong, but I couldn't quite put my finger on what. It was kind of like a structure that from far away seemed to be standing strong, but up close you notice that a bolt is missing so the whole thing could come falling down at any moment.

I hoped that I was just being silly, that everything was actually okay and Doctor Sammy was just calling Dad because she wanted to catch up. The more I thought about it, the more adamant I was that everything was actually fine. It *had* to be. After all, we'd already had our fair share of bad things happen three months ago.

What else could possibly go wrong now?

CHAPTER 3

THE THREE AMIGOS

Parents' Evening. That's what else could go wrong.

With all the weirdness going on at home, I'd all but forgotten about what I would call the worst day in the entire school year. Well, it's a tie between that and Sports Day. I mean, when you are as incredibly average as me, Parents' Evening is just not a night that you look forward to.

To make matters a hundred times worse, both Mum and Dad insisted on coming. On the surface, this wasn't exactly unusual. After all, Mum and Dad had gone to every Parents' Evening together for as long as I could remember. But this would be the first one that they'd go to after the whole Dad moving out drama, which made me dread the whole thing even more.

'I'll be there at four p.m. on the dot, okay, darling?' Mum called from her open car window as she dropped me off for school the next morning. I always made sure she parked three streets away from the Vale Gate High entrance.

'Is Dad still coming?'

Mum rolled her eyes and sighed heavily. 'Unfortunately,' she muttered under her breath, her lip half-curling around the word.

'You don't have to come, you know,' I said, trying to sound casual and like it wasn't a big deal.

'You mean you want your father there and not me?'

'NO!' I said, a little too loudly. I could see tears welling in her eyes, the blue shimmering like a ripple in a pond. She was a budding actress back in her day and she's kept a sense of that *drama* ever since. Her biggest success was playing the third cast member from the left in a small stage production of *Grease*. A framed picture from the show, with Mum blurred in the background, is hung next to the front door. She says it's a fond memory that should be celebrated – Dad says she just wants anybody who comes over to see it and ask questions.

'I mean both of you. Nobody else's parents really go.

It'll basically just be a massive waste of time.' I tend to look at the floor when I'm lying, which is exactly where I was looking when I said this.

'Don't be silly,' Mum said, the tears already forgotten. Her mood could switch like the weather these days, from the brightest sunshine to the greyest rain at the drop of a hat. 'I'll be there front and centre to hear about all the great things you've done this year. I can hardly wait!'

'Me either,' I muttered.

'See you later, honey!' Mum called. 'And please don't shuffle, sweetheart, dreadful for your posture!' My posture, to be honest, was the least of my problems.

Vale Gate High is a hodgepodge of old and new buildings, crammed together to make the only secondary school for miles around. The older parts sag against the newer ones for support and look as if they are one strong wind away from collapsing. Every kid from our town goes to Vale Gate High. Well, unless they fancy the hour it takes to get to the Academy.

As soon as you walk through the Science block of our school and out into the courtyard, you see it – a great mix of kids with barely two looking even vaguely similar. There are the students who have accessorized their school blazers

with enough pins to hide the fabric underneath; the ones who have tried to push the strict dress code and added a flash of colour to their uniforms with jackets and hoodies and scarves; the tall kids, the short kids, the kids who've apparently stopped growing altogether; those who walk like zombies to their next class while others sprint between them. Like every other school, walking into Vale Gate High is like gaining free entry to the zoo, and you never quite know what you are going to see that day.

I was halfway across the courtyard, heading towards my locker, when Caveman Kyle, who was looking in the opposite direction, came barging into me. I stumbled back, already trying to locate the closest teacher in case things took a turn for the worst. But Caveman Kyle was too busy holding a student council badge above his head, laughing like pure evil as the kid he'd taken it from jumped up and down trying to reach it.

Kyle doesn't know I call him Caveman, by the way. In fact, nobody but Seb and Bell know about that nickname and that's only because they use it too. The reason Kyle doesn't know about his nickname is because we call him that behind his back. I got this trick from my mum. She's always talking about Mrs Fielder from number eleven and

Mr Quarterman from number seven. I heard her telling Seb's mum – who's called Sabine – that Mrs Fielder and Mr Quarterman are friends, which seems to be something of a scandal if Mum's smirk and raised eyebrows are anything to go by. However, she doesn't tell Mrs Fielder and Mr Quarterman that she knows they're friends. She just smiles and waves when she sees them together, then goes straight home, picks up the phone in one hand, a glass of wine in the other, and calls Sabine.

Anyway, Kyle is the most popular kid in Year Seven for reasons I can't quite fathom considering he's not all that nice or all that funny either. He was the first to sprout a hair on his chin and someone once told me he had three on his chest, but that was just a rumour. I think it's because of this that he sits at the top of the Year Seven pyramid. Me and Seb are perilously close to the bottom of that heap, but having Bell by our side has boosted our status a little.

Sending a prayer to the skies that the student council kid would just leave his badge and ask a teacher for a new one, I slipped past Kyle and ducked into a throng of passing drama kids. When I got to my locker, Bell and Seb were already there, too embroiled in an argument over a video game to notice my arrival.

Seb is short and slight and always pushing his glasses up his nose to stop them from falling off his face. His jaw kind of juts out a little, but I think it's because he clenches his teeth together when he's doing just about anything. He's the shortest but the oldest and by far the wisest of us all. Sometimes it feels a bit like being best friends with a walking, non-stop-talking encyclopaedia. He never brags about it, though. Not unless he's trying to get one-up on Bell anyway.

We met when we were toddlers, and even then, Seb was smaller than I was. Our mums took us to the same playgroup, plonked us down next to each other and became fast friends, so it would've been weird if we didn't become best friends too. I still hadn't started talking by then, and it was Doctor Sammy's suggestion that I mix with other kids. I guess you could say Seb played a huge part in how I finally started to speak, not least because he never shuts up. Seb talks a lot when he's nervous, which is all the time and something he's definitely inherited from his mum. He talks a lot when he's happy or when he's sad, when he feels awkward or angry or confused. And when his mouth isn't doing the talking, his eyes are doing it for him, darting about like green pebbles that never quite settle. He sometimes hides behind his hair, which flops down into a sandy-coloured fringe that covers his eyes when he's embarrassed.

Then there's Bell. She's taller than both of us, and we kind of look like we could be brother and sister, with our brown skin and full cheeks. She has a small scar above her left eye, a pale pink that slashes through her eyebrow. You can only see it when you're up close. She says she can't remember how she got it, which must mean it came about because of something really embarrassing.

Seb and I met Bell at the arcade a couple of summers ago. She was furiously shouting at one of the screens while shooting a bunch of invading aliens, her hair tied back in black waves so it wouldn't get in her way. We watched in awe as she cleared that level, then the next one and the one after that, her usually soft brown eyes hard and full of fire. At one point, as she neared the all-time high score, she ran out of lives, a countdown flashing on the screen.

'I don't have any coins left!' Bell gasped, watching the seconds trickle away along with her chance to write her name in the machine's history books. I quickly dug in my pockets and fished out my last coin, slamming it into the machine just in time. Bell grinned and gave me a quick high-five before turning her attention back to the game. By the time she'd finished, she'd beaten the all-time high score by almost double and our friendship was confirmed.

She's the natural leader of our little trio, confident and bold, sarcastic but kind. If Seb is the one who's freaking out, Bell will be the one to calm us all back down. She's also super competitive and great at pretty much every video game ever invented, which is what Seb and Bell were arguing about when I arrived.

'I'm just saying that it's an unfair advantage when your mum isn't listing the dangers of mobile phones and how being outside after six p.m. increases your chances of getting a summer cold,' Seb said moodily.

Bell scoffed. 'I had Jack screaming from the next room the entire time we were playing, that's no excuse.' Bell's baby brother had announced his arrival less than three months before. We used to go to Bell's house all the time before he was born. Now, Bell will get out of her house at any cost – Jack's apparently competing for the loudest wail on record, much to her disdain. 'I got you fair and square, just like every other time. I'm starting to think I could beat you with one hand on the controller.'

Seb struggled to turn his stutters into a coherent

sentence even though they'd had this argument a million times before. He glanced wildly in my direction, his mouth opening and closing like a fish out of water. I knew a cry for help when I saw one.

'What's up?' I said, opening my locker and throwing some of my heavier books inside.

'Seb's a sore loser, but what's new?' Bell smiled smugly in Seb's direction while he leaned back against the lockers, clearly exhausted.

'Long night?' I nudged Seb, who looked as if he were about to fall asleep standing up, and gently pulled him in the direction of our form room. Bell shrugged off the squabble and propped him up from the other side, so we were basically carrying him through the doors and across the courtyard.

'I reached the first rank and took a beam to the head two seconds later. A full night's work lost, completely up in flames,' he mumbled, barely picking up his feet as we weaved between crowds of students, none of whom were in a hurry to get to where they needed to be. 'I'm not tired. I'm just broken.'

'How many times do I have to tell you to save the game as you play?' Bell chimed in. Her gloating was short-lived as a Year Nine barged past, knocking me and Seb sideways. 'Hey! Watch where you're going!'

The squabbling about the night before continued as we joined the line outside our classroom but I was too busy thinking of the phone call with Doctor Sammy to really notice. Staring off into space, it took me a minute to realize that the back and forth between Bell and Seb had stopped.

'Long night?' Seb mimicked, confirming that I looked as tired as I felt.

'You can say that again,' I muttered, ignoring the sarcasm.

'Hi, Archie!'

I blushed as Amber appeared, waving cheerily in my direction as she joined the back of the line. I tried to mumble something, anything, that wouldn't make me look like I still didn't understand the use of words. A spluttered yelp escaped my mouth instead, which made one of Amber's friends cackle raucously. Bell rolled her eyes and tried to hide me from view.

'I know you can't have reached the first rank before me,' she said, trying to bring us back to the conversation as we filed into the classroom. 'I've seen you play, you'd be lucky to make it to the fifth.' We took our seats, three chairs lined up next to each other at a table in the back of the room. 'Soooo ... what's up?'

I usually tell Seb and Bell everything, and I mean *everything*. They're still the only people who *really* know what happened to Dipsy, the family hamster, two summers ago, and they've never told a soul that I once scored three out of a hundred in a maths test. I wish I could tell you that total was a result of me not trying. Alas, I thought I'd tried pretty hard that day.

'I'm not sure,' I said slowly, wondering how best to explain that I knew for sure something was wrong but didn't have any concrete evidence to back it up. 'Things are just a little weird right now.'

'Five?' said Seb.

The three of us have a simple code for how bad a problem is. One is the least bad, of course. Five is the average. We haven't had a ten in a while.

'Five.' I nodded. Considering I didn't know what was actually wrong yet, I thought it was probably best not to get ahead of myself.

I quickly explained about the phone call from Doctor Sammy as Mrs Greene hurried through the door, beginning the register before she'd even sat down at her desk.

'Hmm,' mused Bell when I'd finished. Her eyes narrowed a little. She loves a mystery to solve and had recently become fond of diving into books about horrible crimes that made my stomach lurch at the thought of them. 'That is strange,' she said.

'Very,' agreed Seb. 'Have you asked your mum what it's about?'

I shook my head. 'I'm not sure I want to hear the answer.'

'Well, maybe start there and see what she says,' Bell said under her breath as Mrs Greene shot a warning glance in our direction.

'I'm sure it's nothing to worry about,' Seb added, although his face said otherwise.

Knowing Seb, he had probably already imagined a hundred of the worst possible scenarios that could happen. But I'm not sure even he could have guessed what was actually going on.

CHAPTER 4

A VOLCANIC ERUPTION OF
GIGANTIC PROPORTIONS

With Parents' Evening looming over us, the day crawled by with the urgency of a snail. I couldn't tell if my nerves were about the prospect of teachers telling my parents how distinctly average I'd been all year, the phone call with Doctor Sammy and the mystery of Mum and Dad, or an evil combination of them both.

In our fifth and final lesson of the day – Chemistry, unfortunately – I was so worked up about literally everything that I forgot to pay attention to the fizzing test tubes hovering over my Bunsen burner. By the time I'd realized that I was seconds away from setting the entire Science block on fire, they were too burnt to salvage. The heat had turned the test tubes black and a pungent smell wafted around my station. *Great.* Everything was going just *great.*

The final bell should've cheered me up a little, but I couldn't stop thinking about what might lie ahead. Of course, to make matters worse, Dad was running late for Parents' Evening. When he pulled into the car park, a whole twenty-three minutes later than planned, Mum's lips were pursed, her face pinched. She could've been chewing on a lemon, which seemed to be her constant mood whenever she saw Dad these days.

'I'm sorry, I'm sorry,' Dad said before he'd even opened his car door. He held his hands up in mock surrender. 'Bob needed one more file looking over before I left.'

'A FILE!' Mum all but screeched, as if she'd never heard the word before. 'We've been waiting here for half the bloody night!'

'Twenty-three minutes, Mum,' I sighed.

'Oh, that's it, take *his* side!' Mum's voice was now just an octave below hysterical.

'Let's just get inside, shall we?' Dad looked down at me while Mum continued to mutter to herself. 'Ready, Maverick?'

'Do we haaaaave to do this?' I tried one more time.

'Parents' Evening is dumb, and it doesn't even mean anything.'

'Something you want to tell us?' Dad's eyes narrowed as he studied my face. I looked at his shoes, trying to hide the involuntary blush that creeps up my neck when I'm about to be caught lying.

'No,' I eventually muttered, defeated. 'I guess we should just get this over with.'

'Yes, let's,' Mum sniffed. 'I suddenly feel exhausted.' With one last glare at Dad, she turned on her heel and marched towards the doors, her nose in the air.

'I suppose I'd better not tell her why I was really late,' Dad said in a low voice.

I frowned. 'What were you doing?'

'I might've stopped for a double cheeseburger.' He grinned. 'And I don't regret a thing.'

We both giggled but quickly pretended to cough when Mum spun around to see what we were up to. Yep, this was going to be just about as much fun as I had expected.

'You're right, they *are* acting weird,' Bell mused when we finally got inside. 'I thought we'd got over that stage already.'

We stood at the bottom of the Art department stairs, waiting for Seb. Mum and Dad were standing two metres apart, talking to Bell's parents. Her dad had baby Jack strapped to his chest. For once, the baby wasn't making any noise and had instead resorted to drooling on his dad's shoulder.

Bell was right – my parents looked painfully awkward standing next to each other. We'd had the Everything Is Terrible phase at the beginning, but over time, that'd eventually faded into some kind of . . . peace? Sure, things had been far from perfect, but at least they'd stopped fighting like cat and dog. Now we seemed to have come full circle and back to where we'd started. This just made me even more certain that there was a piece of the puzzle that I was missing, or that was being kept away from me on purpose so I couldn't complete the picture.

'I tried to get them to cancel,' I said quietly. 'They can barely be in the same room for more than sixty seconds without arguing.' I wondered if they'd argued when they'd visited the Bakers' house together. It seemed likely.

'My parents can't be in the same room for more than sixty seconds without doing that weird, mushy thing

grown-ups like to do,' Bell said.

As if on cue, her dad wrapped his arm around her mum's waist, planting a kiss on the side of her head. She giggled. Bell blew out her cheeks, pretending to heave. Even Jack seemed to gurgle his disgust.

'So unnecessary,' she said. 'Give me parents who hate each other any day of the week.'

'We should swap and see how long it takes for you to go running back to the mushy side of things.'

Bell studied the two-metre gap between my parents. 'I think I'll pass, but thanks for the offer.'

'I already hate everything about this,' said a familiar voice behind us. When we turned around, Seb looked like he was ready to puke.

'Why do they insist on telling our parents how well or badly we do in school every year?' His voice shook, like it does when he's nervous. It doesn't take much to work Seb up into a panic. He's his mother's son after all.

'You'll be fine,' Bell said. 'Didn't you like, pass Maths early or something?'

'That was Science! And I barely scraped by in Geography this year. Miss Blum is going to hang me out to dry, I know it!'

'You got seventy-five in the last test,' I said in an attempt to calm the situation before Seb fainted.

'And?' he said.

'It was out of eighty!'

Bell rolled her eyes. 'You need to relax, Seb. I heard unnecessary stress causes wrinkles and premature something-or-other.'

'And where did you hear that?'

'Cassandra's mum.'

I snorted. 'Cassandra's middle name is Star Petal, I don't think you should trust what she says.'

As if on cue, the jangle of a thousand bracelets floated down the corridor. Sure enough, there was Cassandra Star Petal Beaumont alongside her mum, whose arm, the source of the sudden racket, looked like it had been dipped in gold. She wore a floor-length skirt and sandals, showing off a gold ring on each of her toes. When Bell hung out at Cassandra's house, she often came back talking about the apparent health benefit of avocados, something which tickled Dad when I told him.

'Students of Vale Gate High!' The booming voice at the top of the stairs belonged to Mrs Jones, our head of year. 'And, of course, parents. If you'd like to follow me, Parents'

Evening is about to begin.'

'I think I'm going to faint,' Seb whispered.

'If you could save it until you see my parents talking to Mr Kennedy, that would be great. He's never forgiven me for saying I thought he had more hair last summer.' Bell shrugged. 'I was just trying to make conversation.'

It turned out that Parents' Evening wasn't as bad as I thought it would be.

No, it was much, much worse.

Things didn't start off terribly. Mum seemed to have forgotten Dad's existence entirely and refused to look in his direction, which suited both him and me just fine. First up was my History teacher, Mrs Clint, who said I was a joy to have in her class. Mum clutched me to her chest at that, much to my horror.

'Nice going, Arch,' Dad said, patting me on the shoulder.

Before we go any further, I would like to take this opportunity to pause and say how much I wish parents would stop patting us. On the head, on the back, on the shoulder. We're not puppies that need to be stroked and told what a good boy they are. If anybody knows why parents do this, please let me know. And parents, if you're

reading this, PLEASE STOP!

The second teacher was Mr Quarterman. Remember him? He lives on my street, at number seven. He's my Art teacher and he's nice enough, I guess. I'm not sure if it's him that's boring or if it's the Art that's boring, but I'm definitely not a star pupil in his classes. Anyway, Mr Quarterman said some nice things, like how I show up on time and, for the most part, pay attention. But just before we could get up to leave, disaster struck.

'So, how's Lorraine?' Mum said, a twinkle in her eye. 'I haven't seen her in so long!'

This wasn't true. Mum had seen Mrs Fielder only yesterday when she had twitched the living room curtains and spotted her and Mr Quarterman outside. Right now, Mr Quarterman was blushing furiously.

'She's well, I think. I mean, I assume so. How would I know?' Mr Quarterman was turning pinker by the second.

'Meg,' Dad said under his breath.

Mum ignored him. 'Of course you would know! You were both outside my window last night!'

'Oh, yeah, that.'

Mr Quarterman looked thankful when Dad stood up

34

abruptly. 'Thanks, Pete,' he said.

'You look after yourself, Peter,' Mum sang over her shoulder as she too stood up.

'There was no need for that, Meg,' Dad said quietly as we walked over to Mrs Greene's table.

'You mind your own business, *Kevin*,' Mum shot back.

'You could do with taking your own advice,' Dad countered.

By the time we sat down in front of Mrs Greene, they were arguing in fierce whispers and failing miserably at not drawing any attention to the three of us.

'And what's that supposed to mean?' Mum said, completely ignoring Mrs Greene's greeting as her voice steadily got louder.

'It means we should talk about this later,' Dad said over my head, trying to smile at Mrs Greene like a volcano wasn't about to erupt in her face.

I sank a little lower in my seat, trying my hardest to send telepathic apologies to Mrs Greene and wishing I were anywhere else instead of between my bickering parents.

'Typical! Start something you can't finish!' Mum all but yelled.

'*You* started it!' Dad retorted, now struggling to keep his own temper in check.

'I did nothing of the sort. Now you're just making things up!'

Mrs Greene looked from Mum to Dad as they went back and forth, neither backing down. I, on the other hand, tried to look elsewhere and pretend that nothing was happening, despite the fact that the whispers had now been abandoned altogether, giving way to something that wasn't far from a full-blown screech. I thought about excusing myself and running to the bathroom, but my body was frozen, paralysed with embarrassment. I briefly caught Bell's eye. She gave me a sympathetic smile which turned into something of a grimace. Amber peered around her older sister to get a better look. Kyle and his mum were staring, slack-jawed and wide-eyed. Even Seb, who was seated a dozen tables away on the other side of the hall, had turned around to see what all the commotion was about. Sabine sat next to him, her eyes darting around with unrest and concern.

'WELL MAYBE YOU SHOULD JUST LEAVE THEN!' Mum yelled, standing up suddenly. She'd started to cry. 'That's what you're good at!'

I couldn't see my face, but I would've bet it looked worse than Mr Quarterman's had. My own anger was only being surpassed by my incredible humiliation, which settled in my stomach like treacle.

Dad lowered his voice, aware that everybody was now looking at us. 'That's not fair, Meg.'

'Don't you speak to me about what's fair!' Mum said, her voice wobbling.

She took a deep breath, collecting herself.

'Sorry, Alison, I won't be staying,' Mum said in Mrs Greene's direction. And with that, she stormed off towards the door without a second glance.

CHAPTER 5

WELL THAT COULD'VE GONE BETTER

Mum was nowhere to be seen when Dad and I got outside and neither was her car. Judging by the skid marks in the now-empty space, it was clear that she had left in a hurry.

'Come on,' said Dad. 'I'll take you back home.'

'I want to go to Seb's,' I said bluntly, not even bothering to hide my anger.

'Archie, I'm sorry,' Dad mumbled, wearing a coat of shame over his shoulders.

I threw myself into the car and slammed the door in response, folding my arms for good measure. How dare they? In the middle of my school, in front of all of my teachers? In front of my entire *year*! It was bad enough that my parents seemed to suddenly hate each other, but this was too far.

'I'm sorry,' Dad repeated. Instead of turning the engine on, he turned to face me. 'That shouldn't have happened.'

I was too angry to put together something that vaguely resembled a mature response. Instead, I went for the obvious.

'It's not fair!'

'I know it's not,' Dad said, bowing his head.

'What's going on? And don't treat me like I'm stupid, I know there's something happening and neither of you are telling me!'

Dad looked down at his lap. 'It's nothing.'

'Stop lying!'

I don't advise yelling at your parents ever by the way. It's usually a sure-fire way to get yourself in trouble.

'Archie, I promise, it's—'

I didn't give him a chance to finish. I was sick of being lied to, of being treated like a little kid. I flung the door open, jumped out and began to run. I didn't stop when Dad yelled for me to come back. I didn't stop when I flew through the school gates. I ran and ran and ran until I could hardly breathe, until I couldn't run any further.

Literally, I couldn't run any further; the road gave way to the beach, which gave way to the sea, and as bad as things were, I didn't fancy swimming the English Channel just to get away from my troubles.

Lungs burning, I sat on a low wall overlooking the water. It was a great place to watch the sun set, blood reds and burning oranges seeping from the sky down into the water.

I don't know if you've ever felt like your parents are lying to you. It's not fun, I can tell you that much. Our parents often think we don't know anything about anything and that we should keep our noses out of their business. Which is fine, I guess, if only they would stop throwing their business in our faces.

'I thought we'd find you here.' Bell sat down on one side of me while Seb sat down on the other. Of course, they knew exactly where I'd be. The three of us would come here with cones of chips or ice cream during the summer holidays, exhausted from hours in the arcades. That kind of joy seemed a lifetime away right now.

'Ten?' Seb said. He'd managed to be silent for an entire minute, which would be close to a world record for him.

'Try an eleven,' I mumbled back.

'It's really that bad?' Bell asked.

I snorted. 'Did you not see them back there?'

'Well, it *was* kind of hard to miss them.'

I laughed, even though I didn't really find the situation all that funny. Bell and Seb looked relieved.

'Are you okay, though?' Seb asked. He sounded more than a little concerned.

I shrugged. 'Dad won't tell me what's going on. He says everything's fine.'

'I would hate to see what not fine looks like then,' said Bell. Seb shot her a panicked look. 'What? I was just saying.'

'It's okay,' I said. 'I'd hate to see it as well. How was Parents' Evening for you guys? It can't have been better than mine, right?' I forced a smile.

'Well, Mr Kennedy hates me and is definitely still holding onto that hair comment.' Bell rolled her eyes. 'He said that I could achieve more "if she only applied herself",' Bell said, punching the air with quotation marks. 'Mr Kennedy's just jealous.'

'Because you have hair?'

Bell brushed a loose curl out of her eyes. 'Well, I didn't want to say it but you can't argue with facts.'

Seb and I both burst out laughing.

'And how did yours go?' I said, turning to Seb when we had got ourselves under control. 'You didn't faint, which I assume is a good sign?'

Seb shrugged. 'Mum finally said she might buy me a phone, although she still thinks they're the devil and I'm too young to have one. But yeah, I guess it went okay.'

'Okay?!' Bell exclaimed. 'Don't listen to him, Archie. I heard Miss Blum calling him her star pupil.'

Seb blushed. 'Something like that.'

By the time we started heading home, night was beginning to fall. It looked like somebody had spilled a cup of black coffee across the sky and not bothered to clean up their mess.

'And what are you three up to?' a voice behind the hedge next to my house said.

'It's talking!' Seb shrieked, pointing to the bush as we both dived behind Bell.

The bush laughed before a floating head appeared above it, a wide grin on its face. 'Oh, hey, Oscar,' I said with a sigh of relief.

Oscar lives next door with his dad, two sisters, a dog and several goldfish. I think they had a cat at some point too. Mum sniffed when they first moved in and muttered something about not wanting to live next door to Old MacDonald. Oscar's what Dad calls a 'good egg'. He's in his last year at Vale Gate High, which should've meant that the three of us were automatically nervous, bumbling wrecks around him. But not long after he'd moved in, Oscar had volunteered to babysit me and he's been doing it ever since.

'Where've you guys been?' Oscar scooted around the bush and stood in the middle of the street, swinging his arms back and forth.

'Just around.' I shrugged. 'It was Parents' Evening. What a great success that was,' I added darkly.

'Ugh, don't remind me. The Year Thirteen one is next week and Mr Yeoman is gonna have my head. He's been waiting all year to tell my dad how terribly I've been doing. And apparently this one *matters* because it's our last one before exam results.' He blew out his cheeks and ran a hand through his already tangled hair. I don't think Oscar owns a brush, but he seems to be happy that way so I just mind my own business.

'Anyway, I best be going.' Oscar nodded back at his

front door. 'The twins are planning their birthday party, God help me. Night.'

We all bid Oscar goodnight and turned to face my own front door, which somehow seemed more foreboding than ever before.

'Are you sure you want us to come in with you?' Seb said, looking at my house as if it were haunted. 'Maybe we should go home.'

I shook my head a little too quickly. 'It'll only be Mum in the house. And she'll have calmed down by now.'

There are a few things I wish I had done at that very moment:

1. I wish I hadn't lied. I was almost a hundred per cent sure that Mum would not have calmed down at all. The truth was, I didn't want to go into the house on my own and face whatever disaster lay behind the front door.

2. I also wish I had taken a minute to look a little further down the street, where Dad's car was parked. He usually parked outside the house, which was why I hadn't

thought to look anywhere else. What a
mistake that was.

3. And finally, I also wish that what happened
    next hadn't gone down the way that it did.
    If you had given me a thousand guesses for
    what was about to happen when we stepped
    inside the house, I would never have even
    come close.

CHAPTER 6

THE ARGUMENT I WASN'T MEANT TO HEAR

I knew I had made a mistake of incredible proportions the moment we stepped into the house. The kitchen door was slightly ajar and, judging by the voices beyond, Mum and Dad hadn't heard us come in. I wanted to call out a warning, to let them know that I was here with my friends and didn't need any more embarrassing today, thank you very much. But the argument caught me off guard, freezing me on the spot.

And it wasn't just blind panic that stopped me from barging into the kitchen. I knew that Mum and Dad were going to keep lying to me, no matter how many times I asked them what was wrong. Maybe this was where I would finally get some answers. The argument was in full swing with no signs of stopping, and it was pretty clear that it wasn't meant for my ears. So, I made my final mistake, and didn't say a word.

The next bit includes a lot of yelling and a lot of crying. It also includes a lot of swearing but don't worry, I've struck that from the record. Sorry to be a fun-sponge, but your parents won't be happy with me if they think I've left them in.

Anyway, the argument went a little something like this . . .

Dad, who already sounded mad:

'**Megan! For Christ's sake, calm down!**'

        Mum, who somehow sounded twice as

        mad as Dad: '**Don't you "Megan" me**

        like this is all my fault!'

Dad: '**It is your fault! There was no need**

to start an argument back there,

especially in front of Archie.'

        Mum: '**MY FAULT?! You think I**

        wanted any of this?!'

If it was possible, Mum seemed to be getting more

hysterical with every word. She was already half-screeching.

Dad: 'I didn't mean it like that.'

Mum: 'I never wanted ANY of this, so don't you dare put the blame on me!'

Dad: 'I know, Meg, and I'm sorry. I could say sorry a thousand times and it wouldn't even come close to how sorry I am. I just ... I had to go.'

Mum: 'I don't want you to say sorry for leaving, that's not what this is about. But maybe if you told Archie the truth, we wouldn't be in this position.'

At the sound of my name, I began creeping a little closer to the kitchen door. Bell tried to pull me back but I shook her off. Seb was rooted to the spot, his face frozen into a mask of fear.

Dad: 'I'm trying to find the right time to tell him! I can't just say it out of the blue.'

Mum: 'If only you'd had the same consideration before you packed your bags and told me!'

Dad, a little quieter now: 'It wasn't like that, Meg.
I didn't know what to do.'

Mum: 'Ha! Well, join the club!'

Dad, quieter still: 'So, what do we do now?'

This was met with a silence that seemed to lay itself over
the entire house, like snow in January. Nobody moved.
My heart was beating so loud and fast that I was worried
it would give us all away.

Mum, whose voice was now back down
several octaves and sounded somewhat
normal, if you could ignore the tinge
of sadness to it: 'I don't know, Kevin. I
really don't know.'

Another silence, this one heavier than the last.

Eventually Mum hiccupped, clearly
about to cry: 'We tell Archie. You tell
Archie. He knows something is wrong.
It'll make everything worse if you keep

this from him.'

The ground beneath my feet seemed to tilt violently, as if the answers I'd been waiting for were pushing up from below to make themselves heard. I tried to grab onto the wall as my mind swam with the possibilities. Was Dad ill? Or maybe he'd done something really bad, like in one of Bell's books. She'd been reading about something called 'fraud' recently and the criminal had been locked away in prison for years on end. Was it that?

Dad: 'I know you're right. I just don't know how to tell him.'

Mum: 'Well, think of it this way – you've already had some practice telling me. Now you know how not to say it.'

Dad: 'Then how do you say it, because I'm out of answers, Meg. How do I sit my twelve-year-old son down and tell him that?'

Mum: 'Well, for one, you need to stop sounding like you're ashamed, that's what Sammy said. If Archie thinks

you're embarrassed about it, then he'll
be embarrassed about it too. Sounding
sorry for yourself also isn't helping.'

Dad: 'Don't be ashamed, stop feeling sorry for
myself. Got it.'

Mum: 'And don't just throw it at him
and then run away. You need to sit
him down and explain it properly. He
might have a bunch of questions, and
I can guarantee some of them won't be
comfortable, but you have to answer
them. And for God's sake let him know
that everything is going to be okay.'

Dad: 'Okay, okay. I'll do it when he gets home.'

Dad took a deep, shaky breath.

Dad: 'Who knew two words could be so difficult to say
out loud?'

Mum: 'Just say it.'

Dad: 'What, now?'

51

Mum: 'No, when man sets foot on Mars. Yes, now!'

Dad: 'Umm ... okay. So. Uh. Yeah. I ... Well, I'm ... I mean ...'

Mum: 'It's two words, Kevin! Hold your head up high and say it!'

So, this is the moment. You know the one; in books and movies they call it the moment that changed everything. It's the little plot twist that you didn't see coming and shapes the story that's about to unfold. In our little story, everybody has their role, and it was Dad's responsibility to put the cat among the pigeons.

Dad, after a brief stutter: 'I'm gay.'

A plot twist I didn't see coming? You can say that again.

CHAPTER 7

EVERYTHING IS JUST FINE, I THINK

'See, there you go,' Mum said, breaking the silence.

Everything was still for a moment. It was like time had frozen. I don't think I could have moved if you paid me. I knew that Seb and Bell were also rooted to the spot without having to look over my shoulder and check. I wondered what their faces looked like, if they looked anything like mine. I didn't want to turn around and find out.

My mind had sprouted legs and taken off, running at a million miles an hour. In fact, it was like every single thought I had in my head at that moment had sprouted legs of its own and now they were all racing in different directions like a pack of sprinters with road rage. There were so many thoughts swarming around my head that

I may as well have had none for all the sense they made.

'And then what?' said Dad.

'What do you mean?' said Mum.

'Well, I don't know. That can't be it. Surely there's something else?'

'I'm not following . . .'

'I tell Archie I'm gay and then . . . I feel like it needs something else at the end. You know, to flesh it out a little.'

'Kevin, this is your thing. Not mine. *Yours.*'

'You're right,' Dad said. And then, 'Sorry. Again. You know, for everything.'

If I were to hazard a guess, I would have said Mum rolled her eyes, but considering I can't see through doors, I couldn't be sure.

'You can thank me by buying me a big bottle of red. Actually, it might take two. Wait a minute, I can show you which one I mean.'

Mum's voice was suddenly coming closer and, with almost no warning, the kitchen door was flung wide open. I heard Seb inhale sharply. Bell actually mumbled a swear word but I don't think my parents heard. They were both staring, dumbfounded, at me. Mum looked like she wanted to lie down on the floor and call an ambulance.

Dad had turned a shade of green so unhealthy, he could've fainted on the grass in the back garden and vanished completely.

The silence was deafening. I could almost feel it, thick in the air and crackling with tension. I bet you can guess who was the first to break it.

'WE DIDN'T HEAR ANYTHING!' Seb suddenly yelled, making us all jump a foot in the air. He looked horrified at the volume of his voice, which was loud enough to call E.T. back home.

'Archie!' Mum suddenly exclaimed. 'In the hallway!'

'With the candlestick?' Bell joked. It was met with yet more silence.

'We should be going!' Seb said, stumbling over every word so he sounded more like a broken robot relaying a voice message.

'Yes, we should,' Bell said with fake cheer. 'Lovely to see you all. Have a wonderful evening!'

'Let us know if you need anything,' Seb said in a hushed voice only I could hear.

Then, beaming manically at us, Bell grabbed Seb by the arm and all but ran for the front door. I couldn't blame them. I would've done the same if I could. In fact,

I nearly did.

So, that just left the three of us. Me, Mum and Dad. All of us silent and staring at the other.

Not.

At.

All.

Awkward.

'Well!' said Mum, just as it seemed like nobody would ever speak out loud again. 'Wasn't that a good evening!' Her mouth curled around the word 'good'. 'We'll have to get you a little treat for doing so well at school.'

I didn't trust myself to speak so I settled for an odd shake of the head which somehow managed to look like a nod at the same time.

'Yes . . . well . . . ummm . . . I . . . have some laundry to be doing!' said Mum, despite the fact there was a pile of folded laundry next to her. 'Give me a shout if you need anything!'

She hurtled out of the kitchen at breakneck speed and up the stairs, leaving me and Dad to stare awkwardly at spots at least a metre above each other's heads.

'Y-you . . . want to sit down?' Dad said after a minute.

'Sure,' I murmured.

My legs felt like jelly, and jelly that hadn't set properly at that. The kitchen table was only four steps away but swimming across the Atlantic Ocean while carrying a whale on my back seemed like a smaller task.

I sat down opposite Dad.

And then I waited.

And waited some more.

I didn't want to speak first and I didn't even know if I could just yet. It looked like Dad didn't want to take the leap either. So, like super mature adults, we both sat in awkward silence refusing to acknowledge the elephant in the room. It was like two strangers standing in a lift together, avoiding eye contact at all costs and wondering how a two-floor journey could possibly take so long.

Just as I began to wonder if some higher power had pressed pause on their remote control to revel in the awkwardness some more, Dad finally spoke.

'Where did you go?' he said in a quiet and shaky voice.

It took me a minute to even realize what he meant.

'Just to the beach.'

'Did you ...' Dad's voice trailed off. He was gripping the edge of the table so hard that his knuckles were changing colour. 'Did you hear any of that?'

I shook my head quickly. If Dad knew I was lying, he didn't call me out on it.

'Well, there's something we need to talk about,' said Dad.

I looked down at the table.

'You know I love you very much, right?' Dad shifted in his seat, trying to sit up straight.

I nodded, not trusting myself to speak.

'More than anything. More than ...' He stopped to think. 'More than beating you at air hockey.'

I half-smiled but still didn't look up.

'I might even love you more than Mum does, but don't tell her I said—'

'I HEARD THAT!' Mum yelled from upstairs, blowing her cover that she was eavesdropping. Dad chuckled to himself.

'What I'm trying to say is that we both love you very much. I want you to know that.'

I nodded.

'The thing is, I ... well, I'm ...' Dad paused, collecting himself. Then suddenly, like ripping off a plaster, he said it.

'I'm gay, Archie.'

He blew out a long, quivering breath, like he'd been

holding it in since I'd sat down. Like he'd been holding it in for much, much longer. Of course, I, who have never really been great at dealing with awkward or serious conversations, had a very comforting and emotional response.

'Oh, okay. Cool.'

Yes, that's what I said. Three very kind and endearing words. Honestly, I should just never be given permission to speak out loud. Dad also seemed to be struggling to decide what to say next, which left another silence threatening to fall on us both. I could've sworn I heard Mum huff to herself upstairs.

'Is there anything you want to ask me?' Dad said. 'Anything at all, it doesn't matter how big or small.'

Sure, I had a thousand questions to ask. But right then, I didn't know how to put anything into words. I wanted to ask if that was the reason Mum and Dad weren't together any more. If it was something he had only recently figured out or something he had known all along. What would change now? Everything? Nothing? I guess I could've used my head some more and actually asked some of these questions out loud, but instead I made the wise decision to cram all of my emotions into a small box, throw that box into a bigger box, and push the bigger box off a cliff.

I knew I couldn't ignore that box for ever. It'd come to the surface before long, no matter how hard I might try to keep pushing it back down. But now wasn't the time to try and make sense of everything, so I shook my head and said no, I didn't have anything to ask.

'Are you sure?' Dad scanned my face, looking concerned. He hadn't planned how this was going to go, but he definitely hadn't expected this.

'I'm sure,' I said. I even forced a smile. I wanted to let Dad know that I was okay, that everything was okay. I just didn't quite know how yet.

'You know you can come to me any time, right? Any time, day or night. If you want to ask me something or tell me something. Even if you want to just sit on the beanbags and play video games all night.'

Mum coughed pointedly from upstairs.

'Nothing will change, not really.' I don't think he meant to sound as uncertain as he did. 'Everything will be just as it was for the last couple of months.'

'Will you and Mum keep fighting?' The words slipped out of my mouth before I could stop them. Dad flinched a little.

'We only fight because we both love you so much. We

want to make sure that you're okay.'

I nodded, not quite sure I understood how that worked.

'Well, if you're sure there's nothing ...' Dad left his question hanging in the air. This was my last chance.

Say something. Anything! Don't just sit there and let this be it!

I stuttered but the words wouldn't come. I just shook my head.

And that was that. Dad stood up to say his goodbyes, putting his hand up high so we could begin our quick, secret handshake. It drove Mum mad sometimes, mostly because she couldn't quite nail the routine herself, but I wondered if she might be happy seeing us nail this one routine without a hitch.

'I'll talk to you tomorrow, Meg!' Dad called up the stairs.

'Don't forget the bottle of red,' Mum chipped back from behind her bedroom door. She sounded a little croaky. Dad waited for her to appear, but the bedroom door remained tight shut.

'Two, I haven't forgotten,' he murmured. He made for the door, head bowed into his chest.

'Dad?' I said without thinking.

He turned around and I launched myself in his

direction, wrapping my arms around his middle. If he seemed surprised, he didn't say anything. After a second, he hugged me back.

'Night, Arch,' he said.

'Night, Dad.'

CHAPTER 8

MUM TAKES THE PLUNGE INSTEAD

I went to bed that night thinking, something which isn't really my strong suit. I have a habit of thinking one thing, which leads to thinking about something else, and then something else, and so on, until I've somehow confirmed that yes, the world is ending tomorrow and hey, it's been nice knowing you all. That night, I unsurprisingly had a lot to think about.

As is now something of a routine, the minute Dad left and the sound of his car disappeared around the corner, Mum re-emerged from her bedroom and came back downstairs. As usual, she looked slightly puffy-faced and red-eyed. She likes to overcompensate when this happens by being overly chipper in an attempt to make me think

that nothing is wrong. That night was no different. If anything, she ramped it up by a hundred and wrapped a feather boa around it.

'What a wonderful evening,' Mum beamed, her eyes still sparkling. 'You make us so proud, darling. Maybe we can pick you up a little something in town at the weekend to celebrate.' She pinched my cheek and I let her without complaint. Were the presents for performing no better than average in school, or a distraction from everything else? I thought I knew the answer but I wasn't about to peek behind that curtain to find out.

'Something to eat?' Mum's voice was so high, it was almost a whistle. She gets this wrinkle between her eyebrows when she's trying not to cry. I saw it then as she looked at me and it made my own cheeks tingle.

Mum busied herself in the kitchen while I tried not to watch what can only be described as a disaster unfolding. She flew around the kitchen like a fluttering bird that doesn't know if it wants to stay put or fly the nest. She kept dropping cutlery with a clatter and apologizing profusely to nobody in particular. When she put the food on the table with shaking hands, it was black. Mum had never burned a dinner in her life, so things were clearly unravelling at a rapid pace. We caught each other's eye and quickly looked away again.

After too many seconds of silence, Mum said, 'Shall we just get takeaway instead?' I tried to smile and she did too. 'Hand me that phone before I burn something else.'

While she ordered us food that I hoped wouldn't be burnt to a crisp, I felt my own phone buzz in my pocket. It was Bell. 'Everything OK?' the text said. I thought about it for a second and then sent back a shrugging emoji. There wasn't an emoji that could come close to describing how I was feeling right then, and I definitely wasn't capable of putting it into words. It was the best I could do because, to be honest, I had no freaking idea if everything was okay.

The food had arrived and been eaten in a ravenous haste (I wasn't really hungry but I wanted to escape to my bedroom without being questioned) when Mum finally took the plunge. She sat in the armchair under the giant lamp that Dad insisted on buying so he could read the books he bought but never actually opened. They now collected dust at his new place, some still in boxes he hadn't yet unpacked.

'Archie?' Mum said carefully.

'Mmm?' Hearts are such traitors, aren't they? No matter

how relaxed you try and tell yourself to be, it will just slam away at your ribcage without a care in the world. It's a huge inconvenience when you're trying to remain calm in the face of an emerging storm.

'You spoke to your father?' Mum wrinkled her nose, like the words had a terrible smell to them.

'Mmmhmm,' I nodded, not quite trusting myself to speak until I knew where this was going.

'And . . .' She let the words hang in the air between us, collecting dust. I didn't know what she wanted me to say so I just shrugged.

'And yeah,' I said finally, when the silence had gotten too awkward for me to bear. This was going fantastically.

Mum untucked her legs from under her, then seemed to think better of it and folded them back in place again. Her eyes were on me, but I could basically see the cogs in her head, spinning. She was making me nervous and the eerie silence creeping around us wasn't exactly helping. It was like the house had been eavesdropping too and was still reeling in shock.

'Is there anything you want to talk about?' Mum tried to smile but it came off as more of a grimace.

There's this weird dance that people do in awkward

conversations they really don't want to have. Not, like, an actual physical dance. That would be strange. But a kind of conversational dance. Mum was doing it now, twirling carefully around her words like one of them might explode in her face.

'Not really,' I said, even though that wasn't strictly true. I had a lot of questions. Tons, in fact. But some things you just don't want to talk to your parents about, right? And for me, this was one of them.

Mum shifted in her chair once more, lacing her hands together and putting them in her lap. She looked even more serious than when she talks on the phone with Sabine about Mr Quarterman and Mrs Fielder.

'I know you might not want to talk about anything right now. Or maybe you don't want to talk to me or your dad about it at all. But you know we're here for you, no matter what, okay? Whenever you need us.' I looked down into my own lap, my eyes starting to burn.

'I just don't want things to change,' I said quietly. 'I don't want Dad to change and I don't want you to change. I just want everything to stay the same.'

This wasn't exactly true. If I could, I'd wish for things to go back to how they were before Mum and Dad hated each other, before Dad moved out. But there wasn't a genie in the world who could grant that wish now, I was sure of that much.

Mum got up and came to sit beside me, pulling me in close.

'Sometimes things change, and that's okay. But you'll always have your dad and me, whatever happens,' she said into my hair.

'Is Dad going to be okay?'

'Of course he is, sweetheart. Why ever would he not be?'

I shrugged and mumbled, 'I dunno,' into Mum's arm.

'Being gay doesn't change who you are, Archie.' Mum held me a little tighter, squeezing me into her. 'Your dad is still your dad. Nothing could ever change that.'

We stayed there on the sofa for a little while, Mum pretending she wasn't crying by coughing loudly to cover her sniffles, while I pretended to yawn as I rubbed my eyes with the back of my hand.

'Remember what I said, darling,' Mum said when she tucked me into bed that night. Now that I'm twelve, she never tucks me in any more. But tonight, she watched from the bathroom door as I brushed my teeth and nearly started crying again when I hopped up into bed.

'You'll always have your dad and me,' she said, pulling the covers up to my chin. 'Always.'

I felt a flicker of comfort at that, but when my bedroom door closed and I was left alone with the dark, those thoughts about everything came hurtling back. They went around and around in circles, on and on, until exhausting questions became restless dreams.

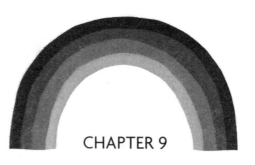

CHAPTER 9

A PIECE OF CAKE

'Should we talk about last night or not?' Seb finally burst out, having gone almost blue in the face trying to hold it in for longer than ten minutes. He looked both shocked and relieved to get it out of his system. Bell shot him a look – well, it was more like a glare or a warning, like they'd already discussed something when I wasn't around.

'I just thought Archie might want to talk about, you know, what happened,' Seb said defensively, tripping over his words and pulling on the cuff of his blazer.

I hadn't seen either Bell or Seb all morning. It wasn't that I was avoiding them exactly; more that after last night I just didn't know what to say. I'd hidden in the toilets until the bell for form room went, then waited some more so that I got into class at the same time as Mrs Greene. I sat between Bell and Seb as she took the register and caught them exchanging a look that they didn't think I could see.

Now it was lunchtime, and I couldn't avoid the conversation any longer. We were tucked away in the furthest corner of the school canteen, our usual vantage point for watching the whole school pass by with their lunch trays. The steady wave of students and teachers didn't pay us much attention as they found their own spots, which was just how we liked it. The only other people at our table were a pair of Year Eights, who were hurriedly passing Pokémon cards between themselves and whispering intently. They didn't seem to be listening, but we lowered our voices all the same.

'So . . .' Seb tried again, ignoring Bell's shaking head. 'What happened?' The words tumbled out in a hurry, like he had too many and wanted to get rid of some. I pushed down a deep sigh and tried to explain.

'And did he . . . you know . . . say why?' Bell said when I'd finished, her forehead crinkling. Even she seemed to be struggling to find the right words.

'Why what?' I could feel frustration mounting in the back of my throat. I swallowed hard but my eyes started

71

to sting instead.

'Well . . .' Bell shifted uncomfortably in her seat, a blush rapidly spreading across her face. 'It just all seemed to come out of the blue is all. I mean, he was married to your mum and she's not a boy.'

Seb tutted to himself. 'Maybe he only just realized that he's . . .' Seb tailed off.

'Gay,' I said flatly. 'You can say it. It's not like the bogeyman appears behind you with an axe if you say it three times in the mirror.'

'I know!' Seb said quickly, blushing himself now. 'Ugh, I'm sorry, Archie. I just don't know what to say without offending anybody.' Bell nodded in agreement.

'Well, nothing is going to change just because my dad's gay. Let's just drop it.' I stood up abruptly, making Seb jump. 'I'm not hungry,' I said moodily, grabbing my tray that was still full of barely nibbled food. 'I'll see you later.' And with that, I stalked away.

This was what I didn't want to happen. This uncertainty and anxiety and what seemed like sympathetic pity from other people. When I said I didn't want things to change, I meant more than just Dad. I didn't want people lowering their voices when they asked me if my dad was gay, like it was a contagious embarrassment. I didn't want my friends tiptoeing around the subject like something foul might blow up in their face if they asked the wrong question. I especially didn't want them to ask questions that I myself didn't know the answer to, which was just about all of them so far.

'Hey, Archie.' Oscar, as he so often does, appeared out of nowhere, his hands clasped behind his back. His top button was undone, a crime that some teachers would award detention for, and his hair was as scruffy as ever. He looked me up and down suspiciously. 'What's up?'

'Nothing,' I mumbled, because apparently that's what you say when there is definitely something wrong but you don't want to talk about it.

Oscar looked me up and down again, then leaned slightly closer to study my face. This close, I could see the freckles dotted around his nose, only slightly darker than the rest of his face, so you couldn't really see them if you weren't looking.

'Nope, definitely something wrong,' he concluded, stepping back and folding his arms. 'Wanna talk about it?'

'No,' I started, but then I hesitated. Oscar is in Year Thirteen, which means he's eighteen and apparently almost a grown-up (not that he acts like it sometimes).

But even so, being older, I thought it was safe to assume he would be automatically wiser than me or Bell, or even Seb, who knows basically everything about everything.

At the beginning of the school year, Oscar also came out as gay. It was big news for all of about three days. Big enough news that it even seeped down to us in Year Seven. I don't quite know why it was a big deal. Oscar didn't think it was, but everybody else seemed to want to make it so.

A week later, everybody had basically forgotten the big announcement and normal service resumed at Vale Gate High. Some people still stared when they saw Oscar holding hands with Dean, but I think that's mostly to do with the fact that Dean's latest hair colour is an icy blue that can be seen from the other side of the courtyard. I heard a rumour that he was almost expelled because of the colour, which was louder than any of the ones he'd had before. But Dean is something of a Vale Gate High gem. They'll probably erect a statue of him in his honour when he graduates. Dean had recently aced a county Maths exam with full marks and time to spare, landing our school in the local newspaper. If anybody was going to get away with blue hair, it was him.

'Actually, there is something,' I said. Oscar looked back at the bustling canteen and nodded towards a quieter corridor in the opposite direction. I followed, my heart in my mouth.

'Well, um, I'm wondering if maybe you could help me,' I said when I finally realized Oscar was actually waiting for me to speak.

'Help you?' Oscar sounded unsure already.

'Well, not help exactly. Just, you know, give me some words of advice.' I looked at Oscar out of the corner of my eye but his face was blank, so I just continued.

'Did anything ... change when you said you were gay?' I kept looking at my feet, concentrating on putting one in front of the other and not falling flat on my face.

'Why are you asking?' Oscar said suspiciously, running a hand through his tangled hair.

'Uh, so, my dad just ... you know.' I dropped my voice and looked over my shoulder for prying ears. 'He said he's gay.'

Oscar sighed with relief. 'Oh, is that it? I thought it was something serious for a minute.' He pushed through the library doors.

'Well, it *is* pretty serious,' I said, flustered from trying to keep up and also at being shut down so quickly.

'Not really,' Oscar said over his shoulder. 'Doesn't sound

like a big deal if you ask me. Just sounds like a big deal if you make it one.'

'But it IS a big deal,' I hissed, even though I was being a hypocrite for saying so when I'd told Bell and Seb minutes earlier that it wasn't.

'Boys!' A stern voice from behind the library desk squeaked. 'Quiet!'

'Sorry, Miss Berry. I'll tell him to keep it down.' Oscar rolled his eyes in my direction and stalked over to the beanbags in the corner. He slumped down in one, sprawling himself in every direction. I took the one next to him cautiously, still annoyed at his reaction.

'It is a big deal,' I said again when I realized he was waiting for me to speak some more.

'Why?' Oscar does this thing where he either avoids eye contact at all costs or locks eyes with you and refuses to look away. Right then, he was doing the latter, and it was making me nervous.

'Because . . .' I trailed off, not quite sure what I thought. 'It just is,' I concluded pathetically.

'If you carry on like that, you're going to *make* it a big deal.' Oscar shrugged, sinking back into his beanbag and looking up to the ceiling instead. He seemed to be

mulling something over and finding it very amusing.

'What's so funny?' I snapped.

'Nothing really.' Oscar smirked, now clearly not trying very hard at all to stop himself from laughing. When he saw my face, he stifled it (with some difficulty) and sat up a little straighter. 'I don't mean to laugh, sorry. It's just interesting.'

'What's interesting?'

'What some people think is a big deal. People love to freak out over things that don't really matter at all.' Oscar was starting to sound all mystical and philosophical and I wasn't quite sure whether I should take him seriously.

'What difference does it make? Your dad, I mean.' Oscar lazily flicked his hand around in the air to illustrate his point. 'He still looks the same and speaks the same and acts the same and eats the same and drinks the same and dresses the same and . . .' He stopped to take a breath as if he had simply been reporting on the weather outside.

'Look, what I'm trying to say is you don't just become a different person when you say you're gay.' Oscar settled himself back into the beanbag and closed his eyes. 'Think of it like a cake,' he said dreamily.

'A . . . a what?' I should've known Oscar would start

talking in riddles.

'A cake,' he said, like it was the most obvious thing in the world and I was the one being ridiculous. 'A big, fat cake that's been cut into slices.'

Do you understand what he's talking about? Because I didn't have the foggiest idea, and Oscar didn't look like he was about to explain where on Earth he'd pulled the cake from.

'The cake, Oscar?' I said, nudging him with my foot.

He sighed softly, like he'd just told me that two plus two equals four. 'Well, when you cut the cake yourself, you never manage to get it in equal slices, right? They're always uneven and one's bigger than the rest and . . .' Oscar opened one eye and saw the look on my face. 'You get the point. What I'm saying is you just need to think of that cake as your dad.'

I didn't know how to say that this was ludicrous and ridiculous and not at all what I wanted to hear right now but, in some sort of a befuddled trance, I just shook my head from side to side, like I was trying to get something unpleasant out of my ears.

'I mean, the cake represents parts of your dad. So, the big slice might be the fact that he's your father. Another slice might be the fact that he's great at computer games or that he's terrible at driving. The smallest slice might be the way he finds reruns of old TV programmes oddly hilarious, or that he has a fascination with outer space and aliens.' Oscar ticked them off in the air with a flourish. 'And so on and so forth.'

I tried not to frown. I really did. But I felt my brows furrow down until they were basically on my chin. I couldn't help it.

'So, what you're trying to tell me is that my dad ... is a cake?'

It was Oscar's turn to frown, which I thought was rich considering he'd started this whole thing and basically opened his own imaginary bakery.

'What I mean is that there are lots of different parts that make up your dad. You know, like who he is. What he finds funny, what foods he absolutely hates. Being gay, that's just one small part. Or,' Oscar winked, 'one small slice of the cake.'

I fought the unrelenting urge to roll my eyes or throw my hands up in the air, which just seemed to amuse Oscar more. I was so baffled I couldn't even speak, so I just pouted and looked out of the window in a strop,

something which obviously really helped matters.

'Okay, forget the cake for a minute, though I personally think that's a great metaphor.' I thought Oscar might pat himself on the back but he just wriggled out his shoulders and carried on. 'So, I'm gay. Surprise, shock, oh my God, blah, blah, etcetera. But I'm also left-handed and a complete chemistry nerd. I love *Game of Thrones* and *Call of Duty* and the colour green.'

I wrinkled my nose because green really is a horrendous colour and I thought Oscar had better taste than that.

'Being gay, it's just a teeny tiny part of who am I. It doesn't change me or make me any different. It's just like . . . a little addition, that's all. It's no more important than the fact that I hate coffee and bubble baths. Do you get what I'm saying?'

I half-nodded because I kind of got the point but I was also still seething about the cake nonsense.

'Honestly, don't worry about it,' Oscar said, awkwardly trying to get up from the beanbag in a flurry of unco-ordinated limbs as the bell for fourth period kicked up a fuss. 'There are a ton of things to worry about in life, and this really isn't one of them.'

'Thanks, I guess.'

'Any time. And don't forget, I've got you on Thursday night. I'm thinking popcorn, home-made slushies.' Oscar ruffled my hair and, without another word, legged it off in the direction of the Science block.

As I made my own way towards the changing rooms for PE, the conversation with Oscar got me thinking. Maybe he was right. I hadn't noticed any difference in Oscar and now there didn't seem to be any big change in Dad either. If anything, he seemed even more regular than usual. The cake was ...

I stopped myself before I could think any further. For once, I'd had just about enough of cakes for the day.

CHAPTER 10

DOES ANYBODY HAVE
ANY QUESTIONS?

The clock had barely drifted past 3.10 p.m., signalling the end of the day, when I found Seb and Bell and mumbled an apology for storming off in a huff. For once, Bell didn't gloat or pretend that she couldn't hear the apology just so I would have to say it louder. We all silently agreed that the minor tiff was better left behind us, never to be brought up again.

As I slouched back towards my house, promising Bell and Seb that I would speak to them later, I picked through all of the thoughts and questions that fluttered like birds around my head. Well, I tried to anyway – my brain had managed to knot them together one by one, pulling them this way and that until they resembled nothing more than a tangled mess with no beginning or end. Still, I gently tugged at random threads, careful not to pull too hard and send my thoughts cascading out all at once. My mum and gran would probably call this 'getting my ducks in a row' but I have no idea where the ducks in that saying come from.

I had decided that one thing was clear – I had been jumping between extremes with little to no use of actual common sense, which wasn't exactly a first. The world hadn't actually fallen down around my ears yet and, for the most part, things weren't really all that different than they'd been before this whole thing. In fact, things only seemed to mutate into something bigger and more terrifying when I thought of them that way. Maybe Oscar and everybody else were right – nothing had to change, not if I didn't want it to.

'I'm not fond of this one,' Mum said in a sour tone as I stepped through the front door and closed it quietly behind me. 'I knew you'd have to get the cheap stuff. It tastes like pig swill.'

'Well, give me the bottle and we'll pour it down the sink,' Dad snapped back.

'You'll do no such thing,' Mum said in horror.

'I'm home!' I announced, more to stop a repeat of what

had happened the last time my parents hadn't heard me come into the house. We hadn't dealt with the first revelation yet; I didn't need a second one anytime soon.

'Oh, *sweeeeeeetheart*,' Mum drawled, breezing through the kitchen door with her curls flying behind her. She crushed me into a tight hug with unexpected force, like she'd just won the Tony Award that she still says she deserves. 'I was thinking pizza for dinner, maybe some ice cream for afters. What do you say?'

'Sure,' I mumbled, trying to extricate myself from the folds of her cardigan.

'Meg?' Dad said pointedly behind her. 'Do you think we could have a second?'

Mum kind of glowed at that, her face lighting up as if a cloud had been filtered away by the sun.

'I need to talk to Archie,' Dad added.

Mum's shoulders sagged, the air seeming to rush out of her like a balloon pricked by a pin. She recovered quickly, tutting loudly enough to be heard three doors down as she rolled her eyes furiously. She blinked quickly three times, sniffed, then fixed a scowl on her face. Without a backward glance, she marched up the stairs, her nose in the air.

'My own house,' she muttered, without caring to keep her voice down. 'Anybody would think he still lives here. Ha!' The bitter tone was snatched away by the slam of her bedroom door. Dad flinched back into his seat at that.

'Arch? Can we talk?' he finally said after too many seconds of silence. He gestured to the chairs around him, one of which was scattered a little further back than the rest, where Mum had been sitting.

I gave far too much attention to which seat I should sit in, more so I wouldn't have to think about the incredible awkwardness of it all. Whereas I had felt optimistic and bright after speaking to Oscar, I suddenly felt like this conversation was about to go south all over again. Dad struggles to speak about his *feelings* sometimes (Mum yelled about that a lot just before he moved out) and I think I inherited that gene from him. We're not really good at the serious stuff. In fact, that's probably putting it mildly.

'How was school?' Dad shuffled in his seat some more. He fiddled with one of his shirt buttons, then smoothed his hair forward even though he doesn't really have any.

'Good.' My attempt at a casually upbeat tone just came off as jarringly off-kilter instead. It echoed in my ears like a taunt. I tried desperately not to cringe but my jaw was already beginning to clench, my teeth jammed together.

'And how's ... I mean is there ... how ...' Dad coughed, his eyes darting around my face but never really looking at it. 'I mean, how is everything here?' The words were stiffer than a plank of wood, which wasn't like Dad at all.

'Yeah ...' I trailed off, not wanting to tell the whole truth. I didn't think Dad really needed to know that I could sometimes hear Mum crying when she thought I was asleep. 'Okay,' I finished weakly.

'I just wanted to ask if you, y'know, had any more ... well, thoughts maybe? Like, questions? Or not!' he added quickly, making me jump with the force he said it with.

I thought of Oscar's cake explanation and studied Dad's face while he fiddled with his shirt cuffs. As I suspected, he looked exactly the same. Sure, the beard was a little longer, but I was pretty confident that it wasn't a result of being gay.

I quickly mulled over all the questions I actually had, burning ones that had been spinning in my head like flipped coins since last night, tossing each aside with hasty abandon and moving onto the next until I could find one that didn't seem too *big* to start with.

'How are you?' I settled with. Dad frowned and even leaned back into his chair, as if the question had knocked him off balance.

'I'm ... yeah, I'm all right,' he said tentatively, like he was expecting a trapdoor to spring open and swallow him and the kitchen table whole. 'How are you?'

I nodded. 'I'm okay,' I said, which, if you ask me, is a funny kind of response because it can really mean anything at all. In fact, when I used to say it to Doctor Sammy all those months ago, she would screw up her nose and politely ask me to 'expand' on that feeling. Dad didn't seem to mind it so much.

The silence loomed threateningly over us once more. Dad actually looked like he might be about to start crying, which alarmed me more than anything. So, I stepped into Seb's shoes and did what he does best – I opened my mouth and talked without a second thought.

'School's going okay although I'm really not sure how I feel about summer holidays coming so quickly because that means it's almost September which means I'll be in Year Eight and that means another year closer to SATs and to be honest I can think of a lot of things I'd rather do than SATS.' That was in the first breath. And then: 'I

spoke to Oscar earlier and he told me I shouldn't worry about what you told me because there's actually nothing to worry about and really you're just the same cake that you were before so this whole thing isn't even a big deal.' One more big breath. 'Right?'

I was exhausted by the time I'd finished with that word-vomit. I fought the urge to cringe at my incredible talent for talking myself into a hole I wasn't sure I'd be able to get out of. Instead, I focused on trying to put a smile on my face that didn't look like I was sitting on a bed of rusty nails. Dad, meanwhile, stared back blankly as if I'd suddenly started speaking in fluent Japanese.

'Oscar called me a cake?' he finally said, almost in horror, which for some reason I found hilarious. I stifled a giggle and composed myself.

'Not exactly. He was trying to explain things.'

'Explain things.' Dad mulled over the words for a moment. I quickly saw things going south and jumped in.

'He says that you're still the same you and not different and that being gay is just a small slice of the cake and isn't all that important.' It had sounded so much better in my head, as words often do, but I went with it anyway and tried to look like I knew what I was talking about.

Dad shrugged, more to himself, his eyebrows knitting together in thought. 'I guess that's true,' he eventually murmured. 'You spoke to Oscar about it, then?' There was an edge to his voice and I began to suspect I'd done something wrong, but I couldn't put my finger on what, so I nodded cautiously.

Dad shrugged again. 'That's fine. Completely fine!' he said, in a way that made it sound like it was anything but. There was enough enthusiasm in his voice to sound at least mildly insane.

'More than fine, actually. One-hundred-and-ten per cent A-okay!' Dad tried on a grin for size to support his 'everything is completely fine' rant but it looked more like a mask you'd see in the Halloween aisle at Tesco. It lasted half a dozen seconds too long and, because awkwardness is the enemy of time, it felt at least double that.

It was as close as we were going to get to talking about anything even vaguely related to what we both clearly had on our minds. I tried to shake the feeling, unsuccessfully I might add, that there seemed to be a wall between me and Dad. But, no matter how hard I tried, it was clear (to me at least, although I'm sure Dad would agree) that it was getting higher and higher by the minute.

The conversation quickly switched to other things that didn't seem all that important before Dad swept me up into a bear hug and said it was time for him to leave. Even then, after months, it still felt weird watching him walk out of the front door and knowing that he wouldn't be back properly.

At the bottom of the stairs, Dad looked up into the gloom, searching for Mum's bedroom door. He paused, like he was contemplating taking the stairs two at a time, but he quickly threw that idea out of the window. Instead, he gave me a quick kiss on the head and stepped out into the early-evening twilight.

CHAPTER 11

A GOLD MEDAL AT THE AWKWARD OLYMPICS

This next phase of the story is something that I now fondly think of as the Awkward Olympics. Actually, fond is probably the wrong word to use. Telling you about it now, I can kind of laugh about it all I guess. But, if I think about it for too long, the whole thing still gives me the jitters. As with most people, I can't stand awkwardness, and yet it insisted on following me everywhere like an irritating gnat buzzing around my ear.

The Awkward Olympics were split into two events, both of which my family excelled at. First, there was The Dinner, which even now I absolutely can't bear to think about. The thought alone makes me want to sit down with great urgency and take one of those deep breaths I hear are meant to be good for you during times of stress. That's what Doctor Sammy says, anyway. Or maybe it was Cassandra's mum. But, since I've already told you everything else so far, I suppose I should quickly explain what happened there before we move on.

It was Mum's idea actually, which was a surprise to us all. It had been a couple of days since me and Dad had spoken about absolutely nothing at all and let awkwardness become our new buddy. Everything still felt unsettled and up in the air, and with exams on the horizon, school wasn't exactly going any better. I thought revising for them might help, but every time I tried to concentrate on a page about some great war in History, or how to say, 'Hi, my name's Archie and I'm twelve years old,' in French, I fell back into the same swamp of Dad-related questions that refused to let me go.

And, no matter how hard they tried, things still weren't quite right with Seb and Bell. They stuttered and murmured around the conversation every time my dad was mentioned. Even if it wasn't directly about Dad, they trod carefully, scared that one small thing could tip me over the edge. I couldn't be mad about it because I felt the same. Instead, the three of us let unsaid thoughts seethe

and simmer into bigger, uglier things. By this point, I was utterly miserable. This was my life now and I'd just have to get used to it, whether I liked it or not.

'I think we should have a dinner,' Mum announced rather grandly and to no one in particular. Since we hadn't been talking at the time – we'd been watching a TV show about cakes and biscuits, which I would highly recommend – it took me a moment to realize that she was talking to me.

'A what?' I said distractedly, not wanting to take my eyes off a particularly delicious-looking Victoria sponge cake. Then I remembered Oscar's take on cakes and it shook me out of my trance.

'A dinner,' Mum said, as if she'd never had a better idea before now. When I didn't immediately react, Mum huffed with impatience and switched the TV off altogether, much to my annoyance.

'Hey! I was watching that!' I made to grab for the remote but Mum sat on it like a petulant child and folded her arms. Parents can be so exhausting sometimes.

'Dinner,' she said again, now struggling not to scowl.

'What about dinner?' My mind was still half on the cakes we'd just been dribbling over.

'We should have one.'

I frowned. 'We have one every night.'

'Archie, please, now is not the time for your smart mouth.' This was rich coming from the person who gave me said smart mouth.

'I think we should all have a dinner – you, me and your father.' Mum blinked quickly at the mention of Dad, which seems like an important detail to add.

I wasn't entirely against the idea in the beginning, which admittedly was bad judgement on my part. What with the disaster that had been Parents' Evening, you would think that the last thing I'd want would be a dinner that included both Mum and Dad around the same table. However, for some odd reason, I actually thought it might be … good? Dinner had always brought us together in the Before Times – it had been something of an unsaid rule that we'd sit and eat as a family every night. And the bigger the occasion, the bigger the dinner. Birthdays and holidays would come around and there'd be enough food to feed the entire street, laid out on plates and in bowls on the living room floor. We'd dive into the treats, stuffing our faces until we could hardly move a muscle, with one of Mum's soaps playing in the background. Of course, those dinners together had become less and less frequent, fading completely before Dad eventually moved out. We hadn't had one as a family since.

Mum threw herself into organising the dinner with enough enthusiasm to fly a rocket to the moon. It was clear from early on that this wasn't going to be any regular dinner. Oh no – for some reason only Mum knew, it was going to be a lot more. Dad had sounded excited for it too.

'It'll be good to sit down together, you know, as a family,' Dad said on the phone the night before. I peered into the living room and saw Mum manically plumping cushions like she was expecting a visit from royalty.

'Uh, yeah,' I mumbled. 'It'll be fun.'

And so the day of the big dinner arrived. I knew from the moment I got home from school, Bell and Seb on my tail, that Mum had gone a *tad* overboard. She'd clearly been whizzing about the place in a tizzy, dusting and polishing everything in sight until it sparkled and gleamed. Now, she was on her hands and knees with a damp cloth, scraping at the already-clean skirting boards.

'Is the Queen coming to visit?' Bell asked, peering around the banister as we shrugged off our backpacks. Mum began fighting a battle with the tangled cord of

the hoover, kicking the switch and thrusting it across the carpet with determination.

'Archie!' she exclaimed, her hand flying to her chest at the sight of us. 'Bell and Seb can't stay for long, sweetheart! Your dad's coming soon!'

Bell and Seb being in the house never usually made a difference to dinner. In fact, before, Mum would've probably invited them to stay and eat with us. Her urgency for us to be alone together with Dad made me instantly suspicious. It felt like we were standing on a very high ledge on a windy day with nothing to hold onto. I didn't like it one bit.

Barely twenty minutes had passed when Mum was shooing Bell and Seb towards the front door, even though Dad wasn't due for another hour yet. 'Let us know how it goes,' Seb said under his breath, putting his shoes on as Mum dived into the living room to retrieve the barely finished glasses of orange juice she'd begrudgingly let us have. She pinballed into the kitchen, hair flying behind her in wisps as she darted about.

'Good luck,' Bell whispered, failing not to grimace.

In the kitchen, there were more plates than I could count, precariously balancing on every surface. There was perfectly sliced bread, steaming slightly after being warmed in the oven. Alongside it was a plate of fancy butter that had no business being in our fridge and had never been a guest at any of our other dinners. I guessed it had been bought especially for that night. Prawns, horrible things that I wouldn't touch if you paid me, were plated up next to a pot of simmering red stuff that bubbled on the hob. There were things in the oven, there were things in the microwave and there were things already on the table. If you'd told me that dessert was thawing on the roof, I'd have probably believed you.

'Looks great, Mum,' I said, having stalled for time in my bedroom so I wouldn't get roped into cleaning the plughole or something just as tedious. I waited for her to turn her back before stealing a piece of warm bread. 'What time is Dad getting here?'

'Any minute now,' Mum said out of the corner of her mouth, hovering over the hob.

As if on cue, the front door opened and Dad came strolling in. He, too, looked around the kitchen as if it were Lapland at Christmas.

'How many people did you invite?' Dad mused, also stealing a chunk of bread while Mum fussed over the fancy glasses that are usually just for display. She laughed a little too hysterically. Dad raised his eyebrows, smiling cautiously as if he were being tricked, and took a spot next to me at the table.

'Dig in, dig in!' Mum cooed, laying the final plates down with a graceful flourish. 'And there's apple crumble in the oven for afters.'

'My favourite,' Dad said, flipping his fork into the air and catching it before spearing a prawn.

'I know.' Mum smiled at Dad in a way that made me feel embarrassed for seeing it, so I made a chore of heaping food onto my plate and pretended not to be any the wiser.

Everything was going just fine – Mum and Dad were acting like actual adults around each other for once and there wasn't a hint of bickering in the air. In fact, Mum seemed to have changed her tune entirely. She laughed at Dad's jokes (which were terrible as usual) and even made jokes of her own (which were slightly less terrible). I didn't want to jinx it but I hadn't seen her like this since ... well, since Dad moved out. It was almost as if the last few months hadn't happened in the first place. A calm warmth trickled over the knots of worry I'd buried at the back of my mind. It felt normal. It felt ... nice. And I didn't want it to end.

But it had to at some point. Things had been going far too well, so I should've guessed something would throw a giant spanner in the works. I just wish it hadn't all gone down before the apple crumble had been served.

I didn't see what it was at first, the thing that fell out of Dad's pocket. I was way too invested in the food on the table to really pay much attention. Dad hadn't even noticed that it had floated down to rest next to his chair leg. Unfortunately, Mum had.

'Ooh, what's this?' she said, leaning down between the chairs and retrieving what looked like a crumpled piece of rubbish. She smoothed it out beside her plate, revealing a rainbow of colours. From my viewpoint across the table, the flyer was the wrong way around. I don't know if you've tried reading upside down but it's incredibly difficult, so I couldn't tell what it said. But, by the look on Dad's face, I guessed it wasn't good news.

Mum murmured the words to herself, but under her breath so I couldn't hear them. Her face crumpled slightly after a few seconds while Dad stared holes into his dinner plate, blushing furiously. Mum's eyes fluttered briefly but, if she was upset, she hid it well under a half-smile. She folded the flyer neatly, and quietly slid it over to Dad, who scooped it up in a shaking fist and stuffed it back into his pocket.

'Excuse me,' Mum said quietly. She stood up slowly, her shoulders hunched over a little. 'I won't be two ticks.' She tried to smile again but this time it wobbled. Hiding her face, she gave Dad a gentle pat on the shoulder, hurried out into the hallway and disappeared up the stairs.

'What was that?' I said, searching Dad's face because I already knew what his answer would be.

'Nothing,' he said, a little too quickly. 'How's the food?'

I was the only one who continued eating after that odd moment. Mum rejoined the table but barely said a word, her lips pressed tightly together. I didn't want to point out the obvious but she'd clearly been crying. Dad, meanwhile, pushed food around his plate aimlessly. He tried to start a conversation at one point, but it ended up falling into the void of silence that was gaping over the dinner table. I also didn't much feel like making conversation. Once again, unsaid secrets were flying over my head, disrupting a dinner that had, for a brief moment in time, been just like before, when Dad still lived at home and the world hadn't suddenly been tipped upside down.

I wanted to know what was on the flyer and what had ruined dinner. Asking Mum seemed out of the question and Dad didn't look likely to give me the answer either. Once again, I was being left in the dark.

By the time Mum remembered the apple crumble, it was more of an apple crisp, burnt black and leaving a horrid stench in the air. That just about topped the disastrous night off, like a sour cherry on top of a foul and unappealing cake.

CHAPTER 12

THE HORROR-THON

As I said before, the Awkward Olympics were made up of two events. The first was The Dinner. The second was a day I've tried my hardest to blank from memory. It's not in my nature to be dramatic – okay, maybe it is a little, I got that from Mum – but this was definitely a day I wish I'd never gotten out of bed for. I can't even look back at it and laugh. I just look back at it now and ... well, I don't want to laugh, let's put it that way.

In fact, I hate to do this, but let's skip the second event, for now at least. I promise we'll get there in a moment but I'm meant to be telling this story in chronological order after all, and that's not what happened next.

The three of us – me, Bell and Seb – were splayed out

across my bedroom, talking in quiet tones about dinner the night before. Bell had made herself a little fort of pillows on the floor, while Seb spun in slow circles on my computer chair, his knees drawn up to his chin.

After I'd told them everything, from the bad jokes at the beginning to the burnt-to-black crumble at the end and all the awkward bits in between, Bell immediately latched onto the flyer, sitting up straighter as she eyed another mystery to solve. Her latest obsession was an author with a name as dark as their books. The most recent one had a menacing skull on the front and currently sat, dog-eared, in her bag. I was almost certain that she'd been taking tips. The last book had apparently taught her to never walk on a criminal's left and to always have a tagline she could use when she'd finally solved a mystery – something like 'Eureka!' or 'Good gosh, old sport, I've cracked it!' Unfortunately for Bell, she had yet to find any suspicious activity to apply them to.

'That flyer *must* mean something,' she said, stroking her chin like the detectives in her stories are always doing. 'If only we knew what!'

'It made Mum cry, whatever it was,' I said, not entirely hating the idea of setting up our own investigation department to figure out answers. Then I remembered the kinds of things that tend to happen in Bell's books and decided that was a bad idea.

'Do you think your mum's, like, upset?' Bell wondered out loud.

'Of course she's upset,' Seb tutted, shaking his head. 'You don't start crying if you're jumping for joy, do you?'

'I don't mean it like that,' Bell said defensively. 'I just mean ... well, she's been quite angry these last few weeks. She hasn't really seemed *upset*.'

I enjoyed listening to my best friends analyse my mum as if I weren't in the room almost as much as I'd enjoy getting my eyeballs scooped out by teaspoons.

'Can we just forget it?' I muttered, already regretting bringing up the dinner. Bell hid her disappointment behind the pages of a gaming manual we'd all chipped in to buy, but I knew she was still calculating something. Seb swivelled on his seat in the corner, vaguely tapping the computer keyboard at irregular intervals.

'Are you sure you're okay, though?' Seb said, holding his hands up quickly before I could twist my face into an expression of disdain. Ever since we'd overheard that argument, this question was becoming as frequent as the

sun rising. As well-meaning as it was, it was really starting to grind my gears.

'I'm fine, Seb. Really,' I added, a little more gently.

'You three! I'm off!' Mum hollered up the stairs, making us all jump. 'Be good for Oscar! And bed by ten p.m., do you hear me?'

'Yes, Mum,' I called back. 'Have fun!'

'And no fizzy drinks! All that sugar can lead to serious health complications in later life. Did you hear me, Seb?!' Sabine called from downstairs.

Seb glared at my bedroom door. 'Yes, Mum,' he muttered.

My mum had decided that a night at bingo was in order after the disaster of the night before. She'd called Mrs Baker from across the road who, like Mum, also needed a distraction (that's what I heard her saying on the phone anyway). Seb's mum was in on the festivities, as was Bell's mum, who'd celebrated a night away from baby Jack by dancing in our hallway upon arrival, much to Bell's horror.

The front door opened and closed, followed by footsteps taking the stairs two at a time. Oscar appeared in my bedroom doorway, grinning mischievously.

'What's cracking, boys and girls?'

'My knees,' I said, shaking my legs out from their crouched position next to the bed.

'I thought we could have a movie night,' Oscar said. The glint in his eye told me he was up to no good. Quick as lightning, he revealed his left hand from behind his back, holding up a DVD for us to marvel at. It was all black except for a white mask in the middle and a small red circle in the bottom left corner. In the other hand, he produced three packets of make-it-yourself popcorn.

'Next up on our horror-thon; a true classic!' Oscar looked delighted, even more so when Bell and Seb whooped in unison. (Seb's scared of almost everything, but horror movies are the exception since they're 'not real life and can't really hurt us'. For that reason, Oscar has stopped mentioning when a movie is based on true events.)

I whooped with a little less enthusiasm. I do like horror movies, I really do. But sometimes I'm not sure if the two-day nightmares that follow are worth it. I still can't look in the mirror for too long after the last movie we watched. And the fact that bad things seem to happen to all babysitters in these films makes me wonder why Oscar is always so excited about them.

'Now, before we continue, what are the rules of the

horror-thon?' Oscar shot us all a serious glare, raising one eyebrow expectantly.

'Horror movies aren't real and we shouldn't be scared of them when they're over,' Bell said quickly, making a grab for the packets of popcorn.

'If we're scared, say so and we can watch something else,' Seb added, clambering after Bell who was already thundering down the stairs.

'And rule number three?' Oscar said to me, giving me a nudge as we followed.

'Don't tell Mum about horror-thon,' I said automatically.

'Got it in one.' I could feel Oscar's eyes on me. 'You okay, little man?' He pulled me into the kitchen and crouched down next to me so we were at eye level.

'Mmmhmm.'

'Sure?'

My bottom lip jutted out of its own accord, which made me feel like a pouty toddler. 'Things still aren't right,' I said quietly.

'What do you mean?'

'I know you said that being gay is just a small bit of the cake or whatever but ...' I thought of Mum leaving the dinner table, and of my own thoughts, still swirling in a

cauldron of confusion. 'It feels like a pretty big deal right now, that's all.'

I thought Oscar might try to use another metaphor to explain it all away, but I was surprised when he nodded. 'It gets like that sometimes, in the beginning.' He shrugged. 'I know I said it wasn't a big deal, and it really isn't. It just takes some readjusting for everybody, that's all.'

'Do you think ...' I trailed off, looking towards the living room door where Seb and Bell were waiting to start the movie. 'Do you think it will get better, though? Like, actually?'

Oscar gave me a reassuring nudge with his elbow. 'Hey, I know it will. I'm living proof, right? Just look at me.' He held out his arms grandly.

'Do I have to?' I joked, rolling my eyes. Oscar held his hand to his heart in mock pain.

'Come on, let's get this horror-thon underway. You'll forget all about your worries in no time when Ghostface starts calling.' I didn't know what a Ghostface was, but it didn't sound like it had any business phoning anybody. If anything was going to get my mind off Mum and Dad, though, scaring myself witless didn't seem like the worst way to go.

When the movie had finished and we could safely look out from behind our blanket shields, Oscar shooed us off to bed. Because he's actually not a bad egg – he's pretty great, but I wouldn't tell him that, his head would get even bigger – he gave us half an hour to play video games. I think it was mostly to take our minds off what we'd just watched. But, before the clock could tick over into a new day, Oscar came up to do his babysitting duties.

'One, two, three,' he counted, patting us on the head with a number. 'Perfect, all kids accounted for and where they should be.'

'I'm surprised you haven't lost one of us yet,' Bell said, burrowing under her duvet on the blow-up bed.

'There's still time, so let's not jinx it before an actual grown-up gets home. Now, in bed and lights off. I don't want to hear another rumble out of you until morning.'

'Have you ever heard of a dictator?' Seb said.

'Aye, and it'll be off with your head if you don't start counting sheep in the next ten seconds.' Oscar grinned. 'Night, guys, sweet dreams. And no getting back up, okay?'

'All right, all right!' I said, tugging the duvet up to my chin. 'We can't go to sleep if you keep talking.'

Oscar pretended to zip his lips together, gave us a double

thumbs up, and closed the door behind him. I counted to sixty, which would give Oscar enough time to grab a drink from the fridge and settle back down on the sofa, before I hopped out of bed, silent as a cat. Well, maybe something a little less co-ordinated, considering I nearly fell over Bell in the dark.

'Adults really are dim,' Bell said quietly, grabbing a controller as I fired up the console. 'I can't believe we leave them in charge of things.'

CHAPTER 13

BACK FOR MORE

Okay, so I guess we have to go back to the Awkward Olympics and to the stepping stone that got us into a whole heap of trouble in the first place.

This time, it was just Dad and me. We hadn't hung out much since the whole big announcement, and after the disaster of the dinner that shall not be named, I wasn't exactly thrilled about the idea of hanging out with both of my parents in the same room anytime soon. So, when Dad reminded me that a weekend trip to Mack's was still on the cards, I clung onto it with all my energy.

The way I saw it was simple. I was almost certain that if Dad and I could just spend a little time alone and finally *talk*, without any prying ears, things would begin to tilt until they were back to normal again. And not just between me and Dad either, but with everything. Maybe if Mum could see things were normal and not-at-all weird between us, she'd be happier too. Naïve, sure, but simple, right?

Except things started terribly before we'd even left the house. Remember how I told you that parents think kids are silly and dumb and don't have a clue about anything? Well, despite Dad's best efforts to pretend that everything was absolutely fine, the minute I saw him, I knew that it wasn't.

He had big, dark circles under his eyes, and his overgrown beard was now beginning to sprout straggly grey hairs. I hate to snitch on my dad like this too, but it was clear that he was in desperate need of a shower. Mum even wrinkled her nose when he walked through the front door, like a wet dog had just trodden mud through the house.

Despite the fact that she'd been moaning he was late – 'No consideration for anybody else's time but his own!' she'd shrilled three minutes before he arrived – Mum whisked Dad into the kitchen as soon as she saw him, telling me to go upstairs and get a jumper because it

was cold outside. I eyed the clear blue sky, the beaming sun, the trees that weren't even slightly swaying in any breeze. Honestly, the lies parents expect us to believe are insulting at best.

'What on Earth ...' Mum was saying as I crept closer to the kitchen door. Of course I was going to eavesdrop – something was wrong and I wanted to know what.

'I told them,' Dad said, barely audible through a thick haze of misery.

'Who?'

'Richard and Phil and ... you know, all of them.' Dad's voice dipped so I had to almost press myself into the kitchen door to hear the rest. 'They came round for poker night. Rich already knew, of course. I told you he'd been acting weird around me and that must be why.' I glared at the front door, hoping Mr Baker would be able to feel it if I tried hard enough. 'The rest of them didn't really know what to say. Gave me a weird pat on the back, made their excuses and left. I thought it might be awkward but ... but they're meant to be my friends. This isn't supposed to matter.' Dad drew a shaky breath which unfurled into a clipped sob.

'Oh, Kevin,' Mum said. My breath caught between my

lungs and my mouth. If Mum was being so nice, this had to be serious. 'Don't you pay them any bit of notice. They just don't know how to react is all.'

'But it's still me,' Dad sniffed. 'I'm still the same person, I don't know why this has got to change anything.'

'It doesn't have to change anything. They'll be back to normal before you know it, mark my words. And don't get me started on *Richard*.' I could practically hear Mum's frown. 'He has his own troubles to be paying attention to, so he can mind his own business.'

Mum cleared her throat pointedly. 'I know you're going through it, Kevin, I really do. We all are.' She said that last bit a little quieter, as if she were afraid to admit it. 'But Archie's going to be down any minute and he can't see you like this. With all due respect, and I do say this in the kindest way possible, sweetheart, you need to get in that bathroom and wipe a damp cloth over your face. And there's some deodorant in the cabinet. Don't use it sparingly, there's enough to go around.'

Dad hiccupped. 'You're right. I don't want to worry Archie.' This concept was rich, I thought, considering I'd done nothing but worry since this whole thing had started.

Suddenly there was the harsh scraping of kitchen chairs being pushed out and the distinct shuffle of a moping Dad getting closer to the kitchen door. I didn't have enough time to flee up the stairs, so instead I stood at the bottom. When he appeared, I pretended to round the banister as if I'd been in my room this whole time. My acting, if I do say so myself, was impeccable.

We stood in the hallway, still as untouched water on a summer's day. Mum peeked out nervously from behind the kitchen door, waiting for someone to say something, anything. Dad looked at the floor, then the wall, the front door and then the floor again, shuffling uncomfortably from one foot to the other. Mum coughed timidly just to fill the silence, which had become the fourth and meanest person in our house.

'Well, have fun then, boys,' she eventually said, after what felt like four suns had set.

'Yes,' Dad said, stiff and hoarse. He sounded like he'd just been told that the world might end tomorrow.

He went to say something else, but seemed to think better of it. Instead, he wrapped his arms around himself and quickly scurried out of the front door without another word. I glanced at Mum, hoping she'd have the answer, or at least a comforting goodbye, but she just looked blankly back, lost for words.

'Try to have some fun, sweetheart,' she said, smiling weakly. 'It'll do you both some good.'

Despite what I'd overheard in the kitchen, and Mum's pleas to pull it together, Dad seemed to be spiralling in the opposite direction. It took four attempts to start the car, and when it finally kicked into gear, it lurched us forward violently before cutting out altogether. Dad slapped the steering wheel hard and blew out a breath while I tried to pretend that everything was normal and as it should be.

The short drive to the arcade didn't get much better. It somehow felt like we were driving to the moon and that we'd never get out of the car, which had turned into some kind of four-wheeled prison. I was surprised when I looked outside and didn't see bars on the window.

'Hope ur having fun. Seb says good luck,' Bell texted as we tried to find a parking space.

I risked a glance over at Dad, peeping out of the corner of my eye at the exact same moment that he did the same thing. We both immediately looked straight ahead again. Inwardly, I groaned. Yep, today was going to be just great.

CHAPTER 14

OUR NEON SANCTUARY

Mack's Arcade has always been our safe haven, our neon sanctuary where the bad, the sad and the awkward get left at the door, even if it's just for a couple of hours.

When I was ten, some of Mum's extended family had visited. She hadn't seen them in ages, since before she'd even met my dad, and she was only meeting up with them now because her own dad was in the hospital. When I'd asked Dad why Mum hadn't spoken to them in so long, he told me it was complicated and that they didn't all see eye to eye over some things.

One of those things was Dad, with his brown skin and huge afro back in the day that made him several inches taller than he actually was. Mum fell in love with him

quickly, but her family didn't. No matter how hard Dad tried to win them over, or how happy he made Mum, nothing seemed to work, and when they eventually got married, not one member of Mum's family showed up. They said they couldn't be there because the wedding was simply too far for them to travel. I once heard Dad saying that it didn't stop them from driving the four hours to see Mum's sister, who'd married someone white.

Anyway, the visit was a disaster from start to finish. It ended with Mum in tears and swearing she'd never see any of them ever again. Dad was upset about it too, but he kept it together. That evening, all three of us went to Mack's and tried to forget about everything that had happened. And it worked! Mum and Dad battled against each other on the basketball hoop machine while I played referee (Mum came out on top, but I have a feeling that Dad let her win to cheer her up), and before long, we were all laughing, the weekend already an unpleasant but distant memory.

What I'm trying to say is that the arcade has always fixed everything, no matter how big or small. Until today. Today was different. From the moment me and Dad walked through the doors, I sensed that even Mack's might not be able to work its magic.

Dad tried to paint a smile on his face but it never really touched his eyes. Every time he tried to say something, his words would stutter and stop on the tip of his tongue, swallowed back down as quick as they'd come. I tried to talk about anything to get us going, to break through the wall that'd built itself up while neither of us were paying attention. I even tried telling the story about Mr Watley's Chemistry class and how I'd accidentally fallen out of my seat in front of everybody. But Dad's stare would fade off into the middle distance and I knew he wasn't really listening. He was thinking about something else that he couldn't shake.

We tried shooting aliens, but our teamwork was suffering and we were defeated before the first level was even halfway done. We raced virtual cars around a pixelated track, usually one of our favourites. But Dad crashed at the first corner and didn't even notice he was driving the wrong way until the computer told him so. Even then, it took him a couple of moments to see the alert flashing on his screen.

Riding motorbikes didn't work, whacking moles with padded bats was a bust, and the dance machine was so far out of the question that there wasn't any point in even suggesting it. We mooched and moped from one machine to the next, game after game coming and going with little success and even less conversation. The sounds of the arcade – the whooping and the cheering of winners, the bleeping of machines waiting to be played – swarmed around our heads. The sounds only seemed to get louder with every passing second that our own silence grew between us.

'How about we try the basketballs?' I tried, seeing two kids shoot their last shot and leave the machine free. Dad didn't answer, looking out through the doors at nothing in particular.

'Dad?' He came slowly back down to Earth, the lights dimly switching on.

'Yes? I mean, yeah, that sounds fun,' he murmured. He reached out towards me with one hand, like he might pull me in for a hug. But he stopped halfway, settled for an awkward pat on the shoulder, and dropped his arm back by his side.

The day traipsed by like we were wading through mud. Looking at the clock, I could've sworn that time was purposefully slowing down just to taunt us further. Even in our neon sanctuary, Dad was entirely miserable.

Misery can be contagious too. It's like a cloud of rain that floats hauntingly from one place to the next, drenching everything it touches.

We were at the air-hockey table, which should've meant that everything was okay. Me and Dad have been playing air hockey together at the arcades ever since I was tall enough to peep over the table and reach the strikers that hover over the surface. Once a week – it's always a Friday – for as long as I can remember, we've come to Mack's, just the two of us, and at the end of each arcade trip, me and Dad would hit the air-hockey tables. It was the best of three and the winner got a point to add to their tally, which Dad kept in the back of his leather-bound journal. At the end of the year, the person with the most points won the Albright Cup, which was really just a cheap bit of plastic with a faded gold star on the front.

But tonight was different to all of the arcade trips that had come before it. There was no hooting and hollering, no competitive (and often lame) trash-talk. Dad barely seemed to be paying any attention to the table at all, missing the puck any time I fired it in his direction. The one time he did manage to hit it, the disc rebounded backwards and slid into his own goal. He didn't even realize that the puck had gone until I pointed out that it was no longer on the table.

'This is stupid,' I muttered to myself. But it was louder than I'd meant it and Dad's ears finally perked up.

'What was that?' he said, trying to hide the hurt in his voice.

'Nothing,' I retorted, slamming my striker on the table and stalking off to the booth where we'd left our bags. What was the point? Things were going from bad to worse and, no matter how much I hated it, there was no point pretending otherwise.

'Don't walk away from me when I'm talking to you,' Dad said, rounding the table. I carried on walking, blinking fast because I cry sometimes when I'm mad and I didn't want to cry right then.

'Archie, I said don't walk away from me.'

'Why not?' I whirled around, sniffling and trying to stop my eyes from leaking.

'Because I'm still your dad,' he said firmly.

'Then why aren't you acting like it?' I regretted it, even before the words had escaped. But I couldn't stop them. Dad looked like he'd been slapped across the face. All around us, people carried on as normal, and I hated them for it.

'Get your things. We're leaving,' Dad said stiffly.

My heart pounding in my ears, I shuffled meekly out into the early evening night. On our way out, we passed the arcade diner, where we would always stop to have a post-match milkshake. Lola would be behind the counter, ready to serve them up in tall glasses with a lick of whipped cream on top. Sometimes we'd get a plate of chips and share them between us, although we'd never tell Mum because she always wanted to have dinner together as a family, back when things were like they were before. We wouldn't be getting milkshakes and chips tonight, that was for sure.

We drove home, the silence gnawing at us in the confined space. Dad switched off the engine as we pulled up outside the house and we both sat still, fascinated by our laps. I knew there must be a telling-off coming. Talking back with an attitude was one of Dad's biggest pet peeves. I'd be lucky if I got back into the house without getting grounded.

But then, while waiting for the hammer to drop, I saw it. It had fallen down the side of my seat, resting between the car door and my foot in a scrunched-up ball that I hadn't noticed before. A corner of it had unfolded itself from the rest, a rainbow peeking out and winking at me. It was the flyer from dinner.

Dad didn't even give me the telling-off I was waiting for. I almost wanted it – at least that would have felt normal. Instead, he gave me a half-hearted spiel about knowing things were tough right now but that not being an excuse for an attitude. It was all the confirmation I needed that we were still stood on shaky ground, and all the encouragement I needed to do something about it.

Ducking and pretending to tie my shoelace, I scooped up the leaflet, immediately blushing with guilt which Dad seemed to mistake for an apology. I mean, I was sorry, but that wasn't quite why I was being so shifty. I didn't know it then, but I had something quite literally hidden up my sleeve that was about to change everything.

CHAPTER 15

THE RAINBOW FLYER

'I have it,' I said.

We were in Seb's bedroom, a small attic room made even smaller by the amount of things piled in every available space. There were big books and small books stacked atop each other, precariously leaning one way or the other and threatening to fall at any moment, as well as hundreds of video games that Seb refused to throw away. He and Bell were in the middle of a furious shoot-em-up, both hunched over their controllers and staring lasers into the TV screen. Neither seemed to have heard me, so I coughed pointedly.

'We heard you, give us a second,' Bell muttered. 'In three ... two ... one ...'

Bell suddenly thrust her thumbs forward on the controller, her fingers flying over the buttons. Seb yelped but he was too late. His side of the screen turned black while golden sparks rained down around a 'winner' sign on Bell's.

'I almost had you!' Seb said in frustration, throwing the controller on the bed. Even though he was angry, he still gave a quick side-eye to check the controller had landed safely on the duvet and hadn't caused any damage.

'*Almost* doesn't cut it,' Bell gloated, smugly putting her controller down in front of her and giving it a little pat for good measure. She swivelled on her butt to face me. 'So, what's "it" exactly?'

'This,' I said, and with a flourish I produced the flyer from its nest in my pocket. A small voice in the back of my mind worried that Dad might notice it had gone, but I clamped the jaws of that beast down as quick as I could.

'It's ... rubbish?' Bell said, taking in the crumpled ball of paper in my hand.

The flyer was even more wrinkled than it had been when I picked it up from Dad's car floor, having been squashed in my pocket overnight. I hadn't dared retrieve it and look when I'd reached the safety of my bedroom, which seemed almost silly now. But whatever it was had shaken Mum enough to make her cry, so I thought I might need backup when I saw it for myself.

As I tentatively straightened it out on the bed, my skin began to prickle, like a sixth sense suddenly alerted to a danger I couldn't yet see. The colours on the flyer had started to fade and one of the corners had been ripped away entirely. It was obvious that it had been folded, unfolded, and bunched back up into a wrinkled ball more than once. Nothing seemed to jump out as something that should upset or scare me. If anything, it was quite the opposite. At the top, in large, colourful bubble writing, it said:

LONDON PRIDE PARADE!

Saturday 10th July 2021

Seb and Bell peeked over my shoulder, taking in the rainbows splashed across the page. There were a bunch of pictures dotted from top to bottom, photos of people paused in various states of happiness and joy. Some were dressed more outlandishly than others. One person in particular appeared to be wearing every grain of glitter in the world on their face. Maybe that was what had shocked Mum so much.

'What's a London Pride parade?' Bell said uncertainly, shifting her head one way and then the other, like an answer would present itself if only she looked at the flyer long enough.

'Maybe there's something on the back?' Seb tried.

I flipped it over and, sure enough, there was something: a map that took up every inch of the page. The roads were made up of simple black lines, with a single rainbow squiggle stretching from top to bottom. There were cartoonish illustrations of landmarks scattered along the route. I'd only been to London twice before, both times with Mum and Gran to see a stage show at Christmas. We weren't all that far from the city, but far enough away that a trip there gave us all a thrill.

I recognized some of the cartoons: the flashing screens

of Piccadilly Circus, the lion statues of Trafalgar Square, the enormous clockface of Big Ben next to the halo that was the London Eye. Places I'd never seen before were sprinkled here and there, including one sketch of a large building with a crown hovering above it. At the bottom of the page where the rainbow squiggle ended, were three words: 'The parade route'.

'I've never been to London before,' Bell sighed dreamily.

'Me either,' Seb said, shrinking back from the flyer like it might explode. No doubt thoughts of London were already illuminating his imagination, setting off every alarm in his head.

'So, how do we figure out what all this means?' Bell scanned the flyer again, searching for answers.

'Maybe this will help.' Seb scooted up to his computer and opened a new tab, typing the words *London Pride Parade* and cautiously hitting enter. We all held our breath, not sure what was going to happen next.

The pictures loaded quickly, chaotically colourful and overwhelming us immediately. It was hard to know where to look first. There were rainbows in almost all of them, flying in various shapes and sizes. Some came in the form of flags and balloons, others wrapped around people to make dresses. One particular man wore a suit entirely pinstriped in all seven colours of the rainbow. It was a bold choice.

'They all look so ...' Bell trailed off, leaning in for a better look.

'Happy?' I said, enlarging one picture where three friends were bent double from laughing.

Seb took the mouse and opened another picture, then another and another. In every one, the crowds appeared to get bigger and bigger, until at one point I was sure there were enough people in Trafalgar Square to populate a small country. But, despite being pushed up against their neighbour like an overstuffed suitcase, every single person looked like they wouldn't want to be anywhere else.

Then one picture caught my eye. I nudged Seb and he hovered the mouse over it, pausing just for a second before clicking. Four people beamed back at the camera, smiles so big that their faces looked like they had been split in half by a ray of sunlight. There were two men that could've been my dad's age, rainbows painted on their cheeks and one arm slung loosely around each other. Their other hands rested on the shoulders of two small kids, clearly twins and no older than seven with rainbows stamped on their arms like tattoos.

'Mario and Dave celebrate their first Pride as a family by taking their children to the parade in London,' Seb said, reading the caption I'd missed next to the picture.

'Wait, there's more.' Bell tapped the arrow on the keyboard and the picture switched to another, this time a man and a woman holding a newborn baby.

'Lucy and Will take their three-month-old daughter to her first Pride parade,' Seb recited.

The next picture was two women hugging, one with an impossibly large and round belly, a 'baby on board' badge pinned to her dress. The one after that: two grandparents, two parents and one toddler, pulling a gigantic rainbow flag around themselves with joy. With each swipe, another family appeared, somehow managing to look even happier than the family before. Then the final picture popped up and I bit my lip hard.

'Victor and his son Junior have been coming to Pride for years,' read Seb. 'They plan on attending many more.'

Victor looked a little older than Dad, while Junior looked a little older than me. He was slightly taller than his father, and leaner too, although you could imagine that Victor had once looked exactly the same. Both had identically crooked noses and bushy eyebrows, although Victor's were two shades darker and peppered with grey, just like his beard.

They were hugging tightly, arms wrapped around each other as they grinned back at the camera. My eyes began to sting as I looked at the picture. Victor and Junior looked nothing like me and Dad, but I could see us in them and them in us and it made me feel empty and full all at the same time. We used to be just like them. Now, we were the complete opposite.

Before Seb could click off the picture, I saw something in the background that sent recognition, a familiar warmth, running through my body. There was a large sign, simple and white, with London Pride written in rainbow colours through the middle. But it was behind the sign that made me lean in close. The window and unmistakable flashing lights belonged to an arcade. There were machines I recognized straight away, and some I'd never seen in my life, but just visible in the corner was one thing I knew all too well – an air-hockey table, with two strikers sitting in the middle waiting for a game to begin.

'I've got an idea,' I said, trying to steady the nerves so

my voice wouldn't shake. Technically, that was a lie. The thought had barely bloomed in my brain, but with each passing second, it stretched further and wider.

'Let's hear it then,' Bell said, hopping back up onto the bed and pulling her hair back into a neat ball, which she tied with a bobble from her wrist.

My palms were sweating. The idea was right there at the front of my mind, on the edge of tipping us all into a great adventure, but I couldn't put it into words. My stuttering, something I did when I was flailing, only served to make Seb recoil with suspicion. He watched me carefully, already not liking what he was hearing. I didn't know how to say it out loud, so I pointed at the computer screen and shrugged.

'I'm not sure I'm following,' Bell said slowly, toying with the flyer.

'Absolutely not,' Seb said instantly. 'Don't even say it.' He looked at his bedroom door nervously, as if his mum could suddenly see up two flights of stairs and through concrete walls to discover what was on the computer screen for herself.

'What?' Bell said, confused and looking between us both.

'I know it sounds crazy,' I started, holding my hands

up. 'But . . .'

I let it hang in the air, still scared of speaking the idea out loud because then I definitely couldn't take it back. Seb was furiously shaking his head.

'This is the worst idea you have *ever* had,' he said, his words falling over themselves in their rush to be heard. 'And that includes your grand sell-a-kidney-to-get-rich-because-we-don't-really-need-two idea! We just can't!'

Granted, I'd had some not-so-great ideas in my time, but I baulked at that because it definitely wasn't one of mine.

'Actually, that was my idea,' Bell huffed. 'And we can't *what*? Will somebody please explain?'

'He wants us to . . .' Seb gulped. 'He wants us to go!' he finished in a hushed and horrified whisper.

Bell looked down at the flyer in her hand, tilting her head slightly. Her face began to light up, slowly at first like it was crawling out of a dark cave, and then forming a smile that stretched from ear to ear. I knew what that smile meant. Bell sensed an adventure, something she was always looking for, and it made my heart beat faster.

'Genius!' Bell said.

'W-what?!' Seb spluttered.

'Oh, come on, Seb! Don't you see what a great idea this

is?' Even I frowned at that, considering the idea wasn't yet fully formed and could still turn out to be nothing short of terrible.

'It . . . is a great idea?' I said.

Bell nodded. 'It sounds like an adventure. An exciting adventure at that.' She looked down at the colours of the flyer, then over to the picture of Victor and Junior still on the screen and nodded to herself again, determined. 'When do we ever get to go on an adventure? The most this town has to offer is Mack's, and with all due respect to our holy land, it's not exactly climbing Mount Everest, is it?'

Seb looked between us both, horrified. He opened his mouth to say something but all that came out was blank air and a couple of stutters.

'Okay, look, I know it sounds a little . . . out there,' I said.

'Out there?!' Seb choked. 'You've both lost your minds!'

'Listen to me!' I hushed, trying to quieten Seb's rising voice. The whole idea would be ruined before it even had the chance to get off the ground if Seb's mum caught us red-handed now. I'd already heard Sabine's lecture on big cities; how they were nothing more than danger wrapped in high crime rates. Every time London or Manchester came on the news, she would start with a knowing snort

and say something like: 'See, I told you, always up to no good in those big cities.'

'I know this might seem a bit extreme. But I feel like . . . like there's this gap between me and Dad.' I looked at the picture of Victor and Junior. 'I don't know. I just thought . . . maybe if we go, we might . . . get back to where we were. I might learn something or . . . I don't know!' I shrugged so deep that my entire neck disappeared. The nightmarish image of our last arcade trip played on a loop at the back of my mind. A wall had been building between me and Dad ever since I'd overheard that argument. The arcade had been the last brick and now it stared back at me, strong and formidable.

Bell couldn't hide her enthusiasm at the prospect – she was basically packing a suitcase full of supplies in her head already. While Seb was happy to stay in his bubble of rules and safety, she was more than happy to pop it every now and then.

'I mean, what could *really* go wrong?' she said.

'Oh, I don't know. How about *everything*,' Seb muttered.

'Oh, come on, live a little!'

'Let me just get this straight,' Seb said. 'You want us to get on the train, all the way to London, for this parade?'

'All the way? It's, like, three stops!' I said, remembering how the journey with Mum and Gran had been over in a flash.

Seb sprang up from the floor and quickly tapped at his computer keyboard. Well, I say tapped – in his fluster, it was more of a Hulk-smash. He leaned in so close to the screen that I thought he might kiss it, then huffed to himself and slapped the keyboard away. I tried not to be smug, but I was glad to have been proven right. We were getting closer; I could feel it.

'It's still over an hour away,' he sulked, crossing his arms firmly.

'It says fifty-five minutes, right there in black and white,' Bell countered, having jumped up to look over Seb's shoulder at the page of train times. Seb blustered even louder and quickly closed the tab.

'An hour's not *that* long,' Bell tried, as if she were talking to a puppy that was threatening to bolt at any moment. 'We'd be back here before anybody even knows we've gone.' She was standing more firmly by the idea with every passing second.

'Do we really need to do this, Archie?' Seb said, switching to me because not only was it my idea in the first place but I am also the weakest link and therefore most likely to cave.

'Well, *we* don't have to do anything,' I murmured. 'But I want to try. If there's even the faintest chance that this could fix things, then I want to give it a go.'

Seb stuttered but couldn't come up with another excuse. Bell grinned.

'Is that a yes?' she said, smiling sweetly.

Seb caught my eye. It was like he was reading my very thoughts, scanning them one by one. We'd known each other for too long to have secrets between us, even if we didn't speak them out loud. If I needed to do this, to find answers, Seb would follow me to the moon and back. Grudgingly, sure, but he'd do it all the same.

He sagged in defeat. 'It's an "if we get caught, I'm putting the blame on both of you and saying you dragged me along against my will".'

'I can live with that,' Bell said, failing to clamp down on her mounting excitement. She looked like a bubble that was about to pop.

'And you have to promise that if anything goes wrong, we come straight back.'

'Done.' I nodded.

'And if something *really* bad happens, we call our parents to come and get us. Even if it means getting into trouble.'

'Yes and yes,' Bell said, checking them off in the air with a flourish and looking eager. 'So . . . what do you say?'

Seb searched my face one last time. 'I guess I'm in,' he sighed reluctantly.

CHAPTER 16

A SHAKY PLAN AT BEST

It was just our luck that our great adventure would have to start at Seb's house. If I had to choose a place to plot and scheme, Seb's bedroom wouldn't even make the bottom of the list, and for one good reason: Sabine. Seb's mum is something of a worrier – well, that's definitely putting it lightly – and even getting her to agree to a sleepover can be difficult sometimes.

'TV off by nine, Sebastian, okay?' she said, coming up to check on us for the umpteenth time.

'But, Muuuuuuum,' Seb whined. Even though we went through this song and dance every time, he still looked mortified about being given a bedtime, especially on a weekend. 'Can't we stay up a bit longer?'

Sabine thought on it, eyeing the three of us. 'Ten past at the latest then. I read something about those wave frequency things that come from TVs. It'll rot your brains if you sit in front of it all night.' Bell stifled a giggle at that. 'Ten past, and that's final.'

Not a second past 9.10 and Sabine appeared in Seb's bedroom doorway, all a-jitter after apparently watching something on the perils of dry shampoo. 'I'll have to throw it all away,' she muttered to herself, tucking Seb into bed. 'We'll be lucky if my hair hasn't fallen out by the morning.' She kissed Seb goodnight, much to his embarrassment, and skittered out onto the landing, closing the bedroom door softly behind her.

'Right then,' said Bell in a hushed and excited whisper, sitting bolt upright after counting to twenty in her head. 'Let's get to planning.'

And so we stayed up for most of the night, conspiring in murmurs that we could barely hear so as to avoid detection, trying to form a plan that wouldn't get us:

1. Caught
2. Grounded
3. Arrested

That last one seemed a little excessive if you ask me, but

Seb was adamant we should add it to the list of possible outcomes as a precaution.

'We can't even go to prison,' Bell objected, shaking her head vigorously as if she were trying to shake the thought loose. 'We're too young. They wouldn't put us in there with the *adults* just for running away to London for a couple of hours.'

Seb snorted. 'Carly Cooper once drank a *beer*,' he said this word as if that were scandal enough, 'and she spent three weeks at the police station. Her parents couldn't afford to get her out, so she spent all twenty-one days in one of those cells. With bars and everything!'

I frowned. 'Who on Earth told you that rubbish?'

'Carly,' Seb said under his breath, flicking a loose thread on his sleeve. Seb had a soft spot for Carly and blushed whenever he was within a three-metre radius of her. Unfortunately, Carly only had a soft spot for inventing lies so dramatic it was almost impossible to call her out on them. She had told some tall tales in the past, but this one was by far one of her tallest.

It was Bell's turn to snort now. 'Carly once said her parents bought her tickets to fly to the moon on Virgin Galactic but had to get a refund because the rocket wasn't

going to be ready on time. The day I trust something out of her mouth, I'll be living in Buckingham Palace.'

'Do you think we'll see Buckingham Palace?' I interrupted, feeling the bubbles of a never-ending argument beginning to simmer.

'Sure. Maybe the Queen will pop her head out and give us a jolly wave.' Bell pursed her lips and waved stiffly to an imaginary crowd.

But Seb wasn't about to be distracted, even by the Queen. 'I was just saying that prison is a possibility and we should add it to the list, okay?' He glowered.

Although he'd agreed to come on our adventure (against his better judgement, he kept reminding us), Seb hadn't changed his tune; not really, anyway. He made it very clear he was nothing more than a reluctant recruit to our rule-breaking adventure and that he still thought the whole idea was terrible, something which I tried not to take personal offence to.

Although I would never have admitted it out loud, I reluctantly had to accept the fact that maybe Seb had a point. We rumbled through plan after plan, jumping from one idea to the next but always seeming to find ourselves back at square one. We weren't getting anywhere fast.

'Well, first of all we'll need a trench coat,' Bell said, matter-of-factly. She had appointed herself as the strategic lead on our planning since she'd done the most reading on the topic of breaking rules (this wasn't a fiercely contested competition considering me and Seb had never touched one of her crime books in our lives).

'A . . . trench coat?' I asked.

'Yes, a trench coat,' she snapped back, as if it were the obvious first step. 'If we're going to take this seriously then we have to look the part.'

'What do we need trench coats for?!' Seb sputtered.

'Trench *coat*,' Bell corrected. 'We only need one. Then we just sit on each other's shoulders so we look taller and more like an adult who's meant to be going to London on their own, not three twelve-year-olds who are out past their bedtime.' She shot a look in Seb's direction. It was a low blow, but he was too busy trying to stop his eyeballs from bursting out of his head to notice.

'Maybe a trench coat can be Plan B,' I offered, not entirely sure it should even be a part of Plan Z. Bell tutted to herself, but she let it go. This was going to be a long night.

What with staying up late into the night – well, it was more morning by the time we crashed – Sunday was basically a write-off. We were too exhausted to even come up with bad ideas. And, when Monday crept around with a new school week hot on its heels, we hadn't got much further. In fact, we'd only just about managed to successfully decide which plans would definitely, without a doubt, *never* work in a million years. After crossing them all off our list, we were still left with a grand total of zero ideas, but at least we knew what we *weren't* going to do. The scrap of paper looked something like this:

- Plan 1: Steal/Borrow trench coat from private investigator. If can't find private investigator, try Mr Watley from the Chemistry department — he looks like he's up to no good at the best of times.

- Plan 2: Ask to borrow Carly Cooper's private helicopter to get to London and back undetected.
    Bell adds: 'Ask if we can borrow her pet unicorn while we're at it.'

- Plan 3: Walk.
    After looking at a map, we have decided that this is not achievable.

- Plan 4: Sell belongings in order to afford a taxi.
    After careful consideration, belongings might not be enough to cover it.

- Plan 5: Commit a LOW-LEVEL CRIME that will get us transported to London for free.
    For the record, and in case Seb's mum sees this, Seb says no and refuses to be dragged into actual law-breaking.

Bell had stuffed as many of her detective adventure books into her school bag as possible, lugging it around on her shoulder as we shuffled into our form room looking guiltier than sin. She set it down on the floor by her chair with a loud thud. If we were really going to do this, we had to get a plan together and fast – London Pride was that coming weekend, which gave us five days to pull ourselves together.

'I've been thinking we should pretend to be other

people,' Bell murmured under her breath while Mrs Greene listed off the latest Vale Gate High bulletins.

'What do you mean *other people*?' Seb said out of the corner of his mouth.

Bell reached into her bag, her entire arm disappearing into its depths as she rooted around for something. It re-emerged with a book bigger than the Bible in her hand. She laid it out in front of us, positioning the stationery pots to try and hide it from the rest of the class. It didn't stop Carly from pausing an exciting conversation she'd been having about an upcoming pool party to peer over at what we were doing.

'I've been looking at people who break the law,' Bell began, purposefully turning her back on Carly. 'Not, like, murderers or anything,' she continued defensively, catching Seb's double-take out of the corner of her eye. 'Just people who do things they aren't supposed to.'

'Sounds a whole lot like a criminal to me,' Seb murmured faintly. He had slipped so far down in his seat, I thought he'd fallen off it altogether. Bell ignored him and leafed through the book, notes scrawled in the margins and most of the pages dog-eared.

'People who go on adventures and don't want to be

found out often pretend to be someone else,' Bell said with certainty. 'They pick different names and do funny things with their voices so they don't sound like themselves at all.'

Mrs Greene cleared her throat pointedly in our direction. Seb looked like he'd just seen the Ghost of Christmas Past riding a unicycle across the room. Bell waited for Mrs Greene to get back to her bulletins before lowering her voice and trying again.

'They also dress in dark clothes, so they blend in.'

'Blend into what?' I said, torn between thinking the idea was kind of silly and also wanting to pick out a new secret name for myself. I personally liked Jupiter Smith.

'The *background* of course. The scenery. It's like putting on camouflage or something. You wear dark clothes and boom, nobody can see you!'

'We're wearing dark clothes *now* and people can still see us,' Seb muttered. 'What else does that stupid book say?'

The argument over our plan continued throughout the day, seeping into double Maths on Tuesday (where we agreed that getting to London by scooter wasn't our best idea) and creating a welcome distraction on Wednesday as we took up our place at the back of a pretty grim cross-country race in PE. Thursday's canteen special – pepperoni pizza and chips – gave us the energy to debate the pros and cons of bringing Oscar into the plan. Seb thought recruiting a 'responsible adult' into the mix was our best idea yet. Bell snorted at the concept of Oscar being deemed anything close to responsible. Let's just say the debate didn't end well.

So, with only two days to go until Pride itself, we still didn't have a plan nailed down. Yep, everything was going to be just *fine*.

Since the dinner, which could be entirely summed up by the burnt apple crumble, Mum and Dad had barely uttered a word to each other. It wasn't like there was any anger between them any more. It seemed that had dripped away, like water in a sieve, until there was none left. In its place was a cocoon of silence so thick in the air between them that it became quite suffocating. Mum appeared to be avoiding Dad at all costs. In fact, when he showed up at our house to drop off something of Mum's that he'd accidentally packed during the move, she pretended to be on the phone so she wouldn't have to talk to him. The lie was a good one, held up by her impeccable acting that had yet to rust. But the jig was over when the phone started to ring against her ear, making it clear that she wasn't having a conversation with anybody after all. Dad had put the trinket on the hallway table carefully and ducked out of the front door without a goodbye. I groaned inwardly, trying my best not to just melt into a puddle and evaporate up into the clouds.

Planning our big adventure, or disaster as Seb tried to call it, was all I had to take my mind off the chilly atmosphere. And what a welcome distraction it was. I dived into the plotting with all the energy I had, not giving thought to what was happening at home or with Mum or with anything else. I was determined to make this work, even if we were running out of time, and slowly but surely, the plan started to take a more realistic shape.

'The train really is our best option,' I said for the tenth time. Me, Bell and Seb were spread out on my bedroom floor later that evening, scraps of paper with scribbled-out ideas before us. Mum had popped over the road to see Mrs Baker, so we were safe to discuss things out loud.

'How much money do we have for tickets?' Seb said, patting his pockets and coming up with three silver coins. 'I've got a pound fifty?' he offered.

Bell dug into the front pocket of her bag. 'Five pounds and ...' She scratched along the bottom of her bag just to make sure. 'Yeah, five pounds. That's it.' She placed the coins next to Seb's in the middle. 'I do have savings but Mum and Dad won't let me near them until I'm eighteen. I wonder if I could dress up like Mum and get the money out that way.'

'Will you stop trying to break the law!' Seb huffed. 'Archie, what do you have?'

I hopped up and grabbed my piggy bank from its shelf. I shook it and the blessed sound of money jingled back. 'Open sesame.' I grinned, and pulled on the stopper. Coins tumbled out in quick succession, gathering in a pile on the floor. The three of us quickly crowded around to admire our riches.

Except ... there were no riches. Most of the coins were bronze or silver; only a handful of them were worth more.

'So that's ... eight pounds and twenty-six pence altogether.' Seb sat back and smiled sarcastically. 'Great, we can get to the end of the street and back.' Bell scowled at his suddenly chipper tone.

'So, we don't have any money to buy our tickets, which means we'd have to hope that the barriers at the station are already open, both here and in London, so we can get on the train.' I scratched my head. A vague throbbing had started behind my eyes, no doubt brought on by all of the thinking. I was sure my brain had never been used so much. 'Not to mention we'd have to pray that somebody on the train doesn't come around asking for tickets that we won't have.'

Seb swayed on the spot at the thought of getting caught red-handed. Bell screwed up her nose. 'If we just followed the plan I said in the beginning, we'd make it to London with no problems at all,' she grumbled, glancing apologetically at the book in her lap.

'What about the toilets?' I said, quickly thinking on my feet as Seb geared up to bite back.

'What about them?' said Bell, wrinkling up her nose once more.

'If the barriers aren't open, we can just say that we need to use the bathroom. They're on the platform and past the barriers, right?' I shrugged, looking at Seb for confirmation that this wasn't another bad idea. He pulled on his earlobe, thinking hard.

'What about the barriers when we get off the train in London?'

'We just do it in reverse,' Bell said, twirling a curl of hair around her finger. 'If someone stops us at the barriers, we tell them we were using the toilet and just need to get back.'

Seb nodded slowly but I could tell he was a little unsure. 'I guess that could work. Although, there's a chance the person on the other side wouldn't believe us and would ask to see our parents instead.'

'If we can't talk ourselves out of it then I guess we get in trouble,' Bell said, throwing her hands in the air. 'What's the worst that could happen?' Seb turned pale.

'Okay, enough about the trains,' I said quickly, trying to distract Seb from his thoughts of impending doom. 'We need to know how to get to the parade from the train station.'

'I already looked it up. Apparently, it's just over a mile from the station to Piccadilly Circus.' Seb circled the landmark on the flyer's map. It sat in the middle of the parade route, the cartoon screens squashed together and fighting for space. 'If we walk, it'll take us less than half an hour. Twenty minutes if we get a shift on.' He nodded to himself. At least he was happy about something.

'Then when we get there—'

'If we get there!' Seb interrupted.

I clenched my jaw. '*If* we get there ... then what?'

Seb started at that, his eyes wide and bulging. 'This was your idea, I thought you had this all figured out!' he said in alarm.

'Well, I ... you know ... I just ... I didn't think that far,' I said quietly. I chanced a look at Seb out of the corner of my eye. He looked like he was about to give birth to a litter of kittens. Bell folded her lips and tried not to smile.

'Well, we'll watch the parade of course,' I tried desperately. 'And then ...' I trailed off. The words wouldn't come, even to me, but I knew there was something there at Pride waiting for us, something that would fix this whole mess. The pictures we'd seen proved that beyond doubt. Magic was on the horizon, I knew it. We just had to get there.

'And then we'll be home by five and nobody will know we've gone.' Bell took over, too impatient to watch me grasp at straws. She looked at Seb, who was now pulling so hard on his earlobe that I was worried it would come away from his head altogether.

'Your mum won't even know you've gone, Seb, I promise,' she added comfortingly.

'Oh God,' he said, wide-eyed once more. 'What are we

going to tell our parents?'

'Well, I was thinking a classic switcheroo,' I said, having already made up my mind on how to deal with this obstacle.

'A switch-a-who?' Bell said.

'I'll tell my mum I'm going to Dad's, then I'll tell my dad I'm spending the day with Mum. They won't be any the wiser,' I said, a little more uncertain under Bell's frown.

'Great, how about we just ground you for a month now since you want to get caught so bad,' she said. Seb fluttered off his chair, walking in small circles and shaking his head tightly.

'What?' I said. 'They won't think to ask each other because they're not even talking!'

'The first rule of lying to your parents: don't keep your lie close to home!' Bell said, rolling her eyes with such ferocity that they almost disappeared into the back of her head. 'It's the easiest way to get busted. Your mum sees your dad, your dad sees your mum, both realize you're not with the other and that's it, grounded until the end of time. Have you *ever* read a book about rule-breaking?'

Seb nodded in agreement. 'She's right, Arch.'

'Fine, we'll think of something else then,' I said, even though I was a little hurt that my grand idea had been shot down so quickly. 'How about I say I'm spending the day at one of your houses?'

Bell sighed and looked at Seb. 'We're going to get caught.'

Seb grinned uneasily, trembling slightly. 'Don't say I didn't tell you so.'

CHAPTER 17

PHOTO ALBUMS AT MIDNIGHT

Seb's nerves continued to rock the boat and, as the weekend loomed ahead of us, we were on the verge of capsizing altogether. The questions were quick and fast, barely leaving room for any of them to be answered before he leapfrogged to the next. Had we left any clues? What would our punishment be if we were caught? Was it really too late to abandon ship and just stay at home?

Seb's imagination had begun to run riot, chaotically blowing every situation up to outlandish proportions. But, even though his concerns got more and more tremendous, they somehow still managed to sound entirely possible. Maybe we *could* end up in prison after all. Maybe London would eat us up and spew us back out again. Maybe we wouldn't be able to get back home and would instead be forced to live as runaways on the streets of the Big Smoke. I tried to push these thoughts away as much as possible, but it seemed like our worries were always just around the corner, ready to pounce on us when we least expected it.

The night before our great Pride adventure came almost too quickly and my nerves were as on edge as they'd ever been. We had somehow almost made it to the big day. Sure, things could still go terribly wrong in a heartbeat, but there was also a little light on the horizon that felt like hope beginning to blossom. Of course, this light could've actually just been a warning siren, but I was choosing to ignore that and believe that it was hope instead.

With a whole day of rule-breaking ahead of us, the three of us had all agreed on an early bedtime so we were bright-eyed and bushy-tailed by the morning. This meant having to awkwardly tell Dad that I didn't feel up to an evening in Mack's. I tried to use illness as an excuse, but we could both hear the lie crackling between our phones. Dad stumbled over his words in an attempt to pretend that his feelings weren't hurt. Our last trip to the arcade hadn't exactly been a success – maybe he'd been hoping that this one would be more like old times.

Seb had taken our early bedtime, which was of course his idea, to the extreme and reminded us at five p.m. on the dot that we should think about hitting the sack, along with a step-by-step plan for tomorrow. We all knew it by heart, but Seb liked to triple-check his double-checks.

I managed to wait it out a couple of hours longer before my nerves flatlined and I fell into bed with an exhausted thump. Mum seemed surprised when she came up to check on me and found me bunkering down in bed already but, with things clearly on her mind, she gave me a quick kiss on the forehead and turned off the light on her way out.

Sleep was as hard to come by as it is on Christmas Eve. I was a bundle of nerves and excitement and panic, all of it tangled together and fizzing like fireworks that were ready to explode in the pit of my stomach. I wasn't surprised when I rolled over and saw that it was past midnight. I was surprised, however, when I realized a light outside my bedroom was still on and somebody was clearly awake.

I tiptoed over to the door and listened but all I heard was the creak of a silent house in the dead of night. So, I cracked the door open a little and listened some more. There was a faint sniffle which was chased away by the silence until I was sure I'd made it up. Then I heard it again and knew something was wrong.

Along the hallway and down the stairs I crept, telling myself with every step to just go back and get in bed because whatever was happening was clearly none of my business. But, like a moth to a flame, I kept going until I was hovering outside the kitchen door. The light was on, spilling out into the hallway. I heard the sniffle again, unmistakable this time, followed by a shaky breath. Somebody was crying. Considering there were only two of us in the house, and I certainly wasn't in tears right now, it didn't take a scientist to guess who. It'd been a while since I'd heard Mum like this.

She was sat with her back to me, looking at something spread out over the table in front of her. Her shoulders were shivering as if she were cold.

'It'll be all right, it'll be all right, it'll be all right,' she said over and over again. Each whisper sounded broken. I moved a little more, trying to lean around and see what she was looking at, and that's when she saw my reflection in the patio doors.

'Oh, Archie! You gave me a fright! What on Earth are you doing awake?' Her voice twinkled with the tears that she was trying to hide. She quickly began gathering up the things before her, stuffing them into leather-bound books with little care. When she stacked the books on top of each other, a single photograph slipped from between the pages and floated to the floor, landing face up for us both to see.

The picture was of the three of us: me, Mum and Dad. It had been taken when I was much smaller, maybe five or six years ago. We were on the beach in front of Mack's Arcade, me perched atop Dad's shoulders, Mum's arms wrapped around his waist. She was looking up at us both and smiling. Mum loves photographs and takes them all the time, special occasion or otherwise. She prints them off and puts them in those books, but only after she's stamped the date on the back and written a message to remind herself of the day. I'd seen this picture before and knew what it said on the back: 'My two favourite boys.'

'I was just going to bed,' Mum said. She tried to smile but her bottom lip trembled. She bent down and picked up the photo, hugging it close to her chest. 'Come on, it's late.'

I went to follow her up the stairs but something stopped me. 'I'm just gonna grab a drink of water,' I said. 'You don't need to wait, I can take myself to bed.'

Usually, Mum might've waved me away and got me the

water herself. But tonight, she gave me a tight hug and swept up the stairs, still holding that picture as if it were a valuable diamond.

But the books still remained on the table, one on top of the other. I'd seen our family photo albums before, of course, but I'd never really paid them much attention. For me, having my photo taken is up there with going to the dentist – it's something I do because I'm told to, not because I want to.

I sat down in Mum's chair and spread the photo albums out in front of me. There were five in total, all different sizes and colours. I flicked open a smaller one, covered in worn black leather. The pages were big enough to house one picture each, although I suspected that there were some hiding behind others that Mum didn't like so much. On the inside cover, she had written 'ALBRIGHT' in neat, capital letters. In slightly smaller, loopier writing, she had written our names: Kevin, Meg and Archie.

The pictures were in no particular order. Some were from when I was really little and still only crawling. Others, slightly more faded than the rest, didn't have me in at all. Those ones were just Mum and Dad, arms around each other and grinning at the camera. There was

me and Mum on our holiday to France, then the three of us together at an amusement park called Fantasy Island. In another picture, we were trying seafood on a beach I couldn't remember. I looked three bites away from throwing up, and I still feel the same about seafood now.

When I reached the end of that book, I tried another, this one big and bursting with more pictures than it was meant to hold. They were stuffed between pages, overlapping each other in their fight to be seen. There was Dad, when he was no older than me. We looked nearly identical, except for that manicured afro, which was the complete opposite to the shorter hair we both have now. On the opposite page there was Mum, her hands cradling the beginnings of a bump. She stood outside our house, Dad on one side in a loose-fitting shirt, a 'SOLD' sign on the other.

The time on the microwave read 01:19 by the time I had finished looking through the albums. Something was gnawing at me from the inside but I couldn't quite put my finger on what it was. The photos had reminded me that we were once happy and whole and not divided behind the walls that we'd accidentally put up. I knew we could have that again, the happiness. We could get back to *us* somehow. And I knew then, more than ever, that Pride had to be the answer. But as that thought looked in the mirror, a different, darker one smirked back. What if, when we got to London, the thing we were looking for wasn't there after all? What if this was all for nothing? The question tried to worm itself further into my head, but I pushed it away. I couldn't think about that now – I'd need all my energy for the morning.

As I stood and stretched, one last picture caught my eye, tucked in the back of the final book. It was me and Dad in the diner at Mack's Arcade last summer, two milkshakes and a plate of chips between us. I had beaten Dad on the hockey table that day, and we'd stayed in the arcade until the bells began to ring and the shutters started to come down. The memory made me smile.

I tucked the picture into my pyjama pocket and piled the books back on top of each other before creeping up to my room. I rooted around in my sock drawer until I found a pen and flipped the photo over on my dresser for something to lean on. On the back of the picture, I wrote 'Victor & Junior'. It wasn't anywhere near as neat as Mum's writing, but I smiled to myself all the same and slipped the picture under my pillow.

CHAPTER 18

A THRILLING AND NOT AT ALL DANGEROUS ADVENTURE

And so, the day had finally come. Saturday. The day I had been both waiting for and dreading in equal measure. I woke up early in a nervous sweat, my heart already racing. I looked at the clock. Six a.m. Way too early to get ready. Way too early to do anything other than sit in the nest of my bed and worry about everything that would almost certainly go wrong. It wasn't too late to back out of the plan, and by the time I heard Mum pottering around in the kitchen, I had basically talked myself out of it altogether.

But then there was that irresistible pull, the risk of doing something forbidden mixed with the thrill of what could be hiding just around the corner. And that void was still

there, the one between me and Dad. It was like we were two islands that could see each other on the horizon but there was no bridge to reach the other.

As planned, Bell and Seb showed up at the house just after ten. Seb looked so pale when I opened the door, he was almost transparent. I thought for a moment I might be able to see the Bakers' house on the other side of the street just by looking through him. Even Bell was a little nervous. She was tapping her foot impatiently, like she wanted to get the show on the road before she could change her mind or talk herself out of it.

'How did this morning go?' I whispered, trying to keep myself calm but flapping my hands against my sides.

'My mum was none the wiser,' Bell said quietly. 'Jack pooped on her this morning while she was changing his nappy, so she was a little too busy to pick holes in the story. Dad is a boy, so he was never going to figure it out. No offence,' she added quickly.

Seb was a little shakier. 'I think she bought it,' he said of Sabine, his words veiled with dread like he expected his mum to pop out at any moment and march him straight back home. 'She only asked eleven questions about the party, but that's better than I was expec—'

'Morning, you two,' Mum hooted, popping her head around the kitchen door, all trace of the night before now gone. The three of us froze like we'd been caught stealing a car. I tried to keep my face straight but I could feel it contorting into itself, grimacing with guilt.

'Morning,' Bell said through gritted teeth. Her hand was gripping Seb's arm tightly. We were about two seconds away from him blurting out the truth.

'Do you want any breakfast? I'm on the granola myself but I can pop some bacon in the pan if you guys are hungry?'

'No thanks, Mum!' I said quickly.

'Well, wait a minute, not so fast,' Bell said under her breath. 'I wouldn't mind a bacon sandwich before we make our great escape.'

Mum didn't pay attention to that last bit, thank God. She just smiled brightly and ducked back into the kitchen. 'Coming right up! I'll call you down in five!'

'What on Earth are you doing?!' Seb yelped as soon as we closed my bedroom door. His words were all mushed together, climbing over each other in their panic.

'We need to eat,' Bell said defensively, sitting on the bed. 'It's tiring work, all this rule-breaking. And if we're going to do this properly, I don't want to do it on an empty stomach.'

'This wasn't part of the plan! We were meant to get out of here as quickly as we could!' Seb was visibly sweating, his forehead glistening. He was pulling on his left earlobe in such a way that it was sure to come away in the palm of his hand.

'Okay, so it wasn't a part of the plan,' I said, holding my hands up to let Seb know that everything would be fine. 'But a little breakfast isn't going to hurt, and the train isn't for another hour anyway.'

As if on cue, Seb's belly rumbled loud enough for us all to hear. Bell smiled smugly. 'Fine,' he huffed. 'But no more breaking away from the plan, okay?!'

'Aye aye, Captain,' said Bell.

I might have thought that the bacon sandwiches weren't going to derail us and our air-tight, not-at-all-shaky plan. In fact, I might have actually thought that the bacon sandwiches were a great idea. It will probably come as no surprise to you then that they were actually the complete opposite.

You see, I hadn't anticipated the actual eating of the bacon sandwiches and neither had Bell. Of course, we both know how to eat a bacon sandwich: one bite, two bites, then inhale the rest. But neither of us had thought about *where* we would eat. When we walked into the kitchen, there was one big plate, piled high with enough bacon sandwiches to feed a small country. Next to the big plate were three smaller ones, clearly for me, Bell and Seb. Next to those was Mum's bowl of granola and her steaming cup of tea.

'Do we have to eat down here?' I said without thinking, looking at the table in horror and guessing how long it would take for one of us to drop us in the glue.

A flash of hurt crossed Mum's face. 'I just thought it would be nice is all. But you can take them up to your room if you want.' She had recovered quickly but I had already seen that look. The thought of last night, of Mum at the kitchen table, floated into my thoughts like a rain cloud, and that was enough for me to change my mind.

'No, it's fine. We'll sit down here,' I mumbled, taking a seat. I looked apologetically at Bell and Seb, who were standing in the doorway, staring in disbelief. Bell gave a pointed nod at Seb before sitting down herself.

'We're so grounded,' she whispered behind her hand. 'It's fine, I didn't like freedom that much anyway.'

Within seconds of sitting down, Seb had already knocked over a glass of water and nearly sent the plate of bacon sandwiches tumbling to the floor.

'I'm sorry! I'm sorry!' he squealed.

'Don't be silly,' Mum said, ruffling his hair. 'Just an accident. But do please try to keep the bacon sandwiches on the table. I would hate to see all that go in the bin.'

Seb laughed tightly. By my estimation, he was turning a deeper shade of green every ten seconds. One more minute and he would be the colour of cough and cold snot.

'So, what do you have planned for the day? Anything fun and exciting?' Mum sat down next to Bell and opposite Seb. We couldn't have planned for this to be any worse if we tried. With Seb directly in Mum's eyeline, we definitely weren't going to make it out of the front door, never mind to the train station.

'Oh, you know, just stuff,' I said, trying to sound nonchalant. Judging by Bell's expression, I was doing a terrible job.

'We're going to the arcade for a bit,' Bell said, jumping in to save us all. 'And then Carmen is having some friends over for a pool party.'

'Carmen? I haven't seen her in a long time,' Mum said, looking immediately at me for an answer.

Carmen went to our primary school, but she was something of a child prodigy. While nearly everybody

else chose to go to Vale Gate High, there was no question that Carmen would end up at the Academy. If you believed her gloating parents, she was three steps away from curing several terminal illnesses and she wasn't even a teenager yet.

Anyway, Carmen was part of our plan, whether she knew that or not (she definitely didn't). We figured we needed a reason to be further away from home than usual, so if something went wrong or our parents called, we'd have more than ten minutes to get ourselves home. After Carmen was accepted into the Academy, her family had moved to Hampton Gardens, a fancy suburb just outside town. When we overheard Carly talking about a pool party in form room – most likely another of her tall tales – it struck us as the perfect excuse.

'Yeah, Carmen invited us to a pool party,' I said, repeating Bell's line so as not to wander off script.

'And you weren't going to tell me about this?' Mum said, her eyebrows knitting together into a frown.

'Uhhh ...' I said, looking down at the table as my face began to burn.

'It was a last-minute invite,' Bell said confidently. 'We only got the invite yesterday.'

'Doesn't Carmen live in Hampton Gardens? That's quite far away, love. How are you getting there?' Mum said, turning her attention back to me. It felt like a scorching hot spotlight was dangling over my head while a neon sign with the words 'HE'S LYING' flashed behind me. Since gawking at my mum in befuddlement didn't count as any form of answer, Bell jumped in to save me once more.

'We're catching a ride with Tish. She has a seven-seater and her mum promised to drop us off and then pick us up again.'

The worst part of all this was the fact that we'd gone over this plan a hundred times already. All we had to do was 'follow the script' as Seb kept saying. We had carefully picked out a good lie, cropped off any loose ends, and wrapped it all up in a bow that, nine times out of ten, wouldn't get us caught. Bell and Seb had already spun the web for their own parents without a hitch. But now here I was, under the microscope and beginning to crumble. That one-out-of-ten chance had suddenly boosted its odds. Thank God for Bell, but the Mum wall wasn't breaking down so easily.

'I didn't think you liked Tish any more, Archie?' Mum made sure to direct her question at me by name this time so Bell couldn't jump in and save the day.

'I do!' I said a little too quickly.

'Didn't she steal your pencil case with all your brand-new pens in on the first day of Year Five?'

'Mum! That was years ago!'

'Hmm,' said Mum disapprovingly, pursing her lips.

I don't know if you've noticed this too, but parents rarely forget a grudge when it comes to their kids. I could count on the fingers of two hands the number of people who my mum and dad didn't like because of something they had done to me years before. I never personally kept the grudge that long, but they certainly did. Dad still insisted that Harry Dempster had purposefully tripped me over on Sports Day when we were in Year Four just so he could win.

Although she hadn't moved from her seat, it seemed like Mum was bearing down on the three of us, circling our lies, chewing them up and spitting them back out. Seb wasn't the only one in dire panic – I was sweating, head pounding and heart racing. We were done for and we hadn't even made it out of the house.

'Those are lovely earrings,' Bell suddenly said with a sweet smile on her face.

Good tactic, Bell, I thought to myself. *A compliment or two will get us out of here in no time.* Sure enough, Mum's face immediately shifted as a grin that could light up three cities spread from one ear to the other.

'I bought them for myself the other day,' she said delightedly, and right then I knew we were safe. I breathed a sigh of relief. We'd leapt over the first hurdle, and I foolishly hoped that there wouldn't be many more.

Seb pointed desperately towards the kitchen door, practically bouncing on his chair with nerves as Mum cleared away the plates. I looked at the clock. It was already half ten and the train was due to leave not long after eleven. We were running behind schedule because of Mum's incessant questioning.

'We're going to head off, Mum,' I said, hopping up from my chair as Bell and Seb did the same. 'I won't be home too late, promise.'

'Stay safe, please!' Mum called to our retreating backs. We tried to walk casually, like we had nowhere pressing to be, but we were doing a terrible job and instead jostled each other to get out into the hallway first and away from Mum's inquisition. We'd almost made it. Our adventure was revving back to life!

Then Mum suddenly appeared in the kitchen doorway, a frown on her face. My insides turned to ice.

'Aren't you forgetting something?' she asked, eyes narrow and curious.

'Ummm ... no?' I said hopefully, beginning to panic all over again.

'Your swimming trunks, silly! You can't go to a pool party without them.'

'Oh, yeah, of course,' I mumbled, trying to hide the cool flood of relief washing over me.

'You would forget your head if it wasn't screwed on!'

I raced up the stairs, wiping sweat from my brow with a pair of trunks from my top drawer before stuffing them into my rucksack and joining the others. Mum was watching the three of us carefully. She was suspicious, and we weren't exactly doing a good job of making it look like we didn't have anything to hide.

'You three are looking very shifty,' she said slowly.

I felt the blood rush from my face. Out of the corner of my eye, Seb wobbled on his feet a little. But before he could hit the deck, the phone rang. Immediately, Mum pounced on it and, within half a second, she'd begun telling whoever it was on the other end about seeing Mr

Quarterman and Mrs Fielder the night before.

'Have fun, kids,' Mum called.

The three of us stepped out into the sun and all breathed a sigh of relief. The day was about to begin.

CHAPTER 19

ANOTHER UNPLANNED OBSTACLE

Now that we had escaped the confines of my house, and the unplanned obstacle of a curious mother, the plan seemed simple enough. Yes, the plotting had started out way more confusing, but after condensing it down to the basics, the plan looked like this:

1. Get to the station and board the 11:13 train to London.

2. If all went according to plan, we would arrive in the city before midday, which meant that the journey was much quicker than any of us had thought, giving us the false impression that we weren't as far away

from home as we actually were.

3. Once off the train safely, we'd wait for the bus at a stop just outside the exit. Seb didn't like the idea of being on public transport without responsible adults, so Plan B was to walk from the station to the parade instead. It wasn't too long a walk, but we'd decided to cross that bridge when we got to it.

4. Once we arrived at Pride, the plan got a little murky, mostly because me, Bell and Seb didn't really know what to expect when we got there. So, this part of the plan just said, rather vaguely, 'watch parade and hunt for clues to fix things'. I had crossed out Seb's addition of 'and hope for the best'. It seemed negative.

5. We couldn't quite decide on how long we should stay at Pride, but Seb, of course, wanted to get back home as quickly as possible. Therefore, we concluded that seeing the parade for an hour or so would be

time enough before reversing the plan and heading back home.

6. REMEMBER THE LIE!!!! This didn't just end the moment we touched back down at home. If our parents asked us how our day had been, or asked about Tish, or some time in the future said 'remember when you went to Carmen's pool party', we had to remember the lie. Bell (and her books) had been pretty adamant about this. It would be just our luck to execute the plan perfectly, only to be busted three weeks down the line when we forgot our cover story.

So, yes, the plan was in place. And yes, there were still a lot of things that could go wrong. And yes, we were all a little terrified, even if we weren't saying it out loud. But we were also buzzing with adrenaline and a small spark of excitement that was growing bigger by the minute. Well, I was excited anyway. I'm not sure you could say the same about Seb.

'I can't believe we're doing this,' he said in a daze as we made our way to the train station. 'Like, we're *actually* going to do this.'

'But just think how much FUN it's going to be!' Bell had a bounce in her step now.

'Parents really are a little dim, aren't they?' I said. Confidence had risen from the ashes of my earlier fear in the kitchen – I knew if we'd made it this far, things were going to fall into place just fine. 'I can't believe they call adults the responsible ones!'

I laughed to the others over my shoulder and was somewhat surprised when they looked back in horror. I turned around a little too late and crashed into someone else, who let out a swear word I definitely can't repeat.

'My foot!' yelled a voice I definitely recognized. 'Archie? What on Earth are you doing?'

'Oh ... uh ... hi, Dad,' I said. I felt my eyebrows shoot up off my face involuntarily. He definitely wasn't a part of the plan.

'Haven't I taught you better than to be walking down the street not paying attention to where you're going?'

'Yeah, sorry, I was just ... I ...' My head was suddenly clouding up with a dense fog that was blindfolding my common sense. We needed to make a move and fast – we were already running late.

'Where are you going anyway?' Dad said, looking at

Seb, who was definitely on the verge of breaking down and begging for forgiveness.

'The arcade,' I said automatically.

Dad frowned. 'The arcade is that way,' he said, pointing over my shoulder. I groaned inwardly. Why was everything determined to work against us today?

'We're going to the shops first,' Bell said, stepping forward and slightly in front of Seb to hide him from view.

'Oh, what for? Buying me anything nice?' Dad grinned in my direction. I returned it with a guilt-ridden grimace.

'Goggles,' Bell said, thinking on the spot.

'Goggles? What do you need those for?'

'Well, to help us see underwater of course,' Bell said, as if it were obvious.

'And why do you need to see underwater? You're going to the arcade.'

Bell wavered and stuttered a little. She stepped back, taking Seb with her. 'You're up,' she said out of the corner of her mouth.

'We're going to Tish's pool party,' I said, trying to touch back down on the solid ground of our plan. 'We need goggles for that.'

Dad looked as if he were about to say something but a quick glance at his watch made his jaw clench. He clasped his hands together, looking up and then down the street as if he didn't want to be caught doing something. 'I best be off, things to do,' he said in a distracted hurry. 'Stay safe by the pool, okay?'

I didn't even need to nod – Dad whipped around on his heel and almost bounded off up the street. I breathed a sigh of relief.

'You FOOL!' Seb yelped when we were safely two streets away.

'Huh? What did I do? I got us out of there, didn't I?' I folded my arms defensively, already beginning to panic.

'Tish's pool party?' Bell said, rolling her eyes. 'It's meant to be *Carmen's* pool party, remember?'

'Oh ... yeah,' I mumbled. 'Oh well, what difference does it make?'

'Let me tell you what difference it makes,' Seb said, wheeling around in a hurricane of rage. 'If your dad sees your mum today and they happen to bring up the pool party, they'll realize you're lying! Then we're all done for. Grounded for an entire summer! We'll probably never see the light of day again until our sixteenth birthdays!'

Even Bell, whose own parents were much more laid back (and focused on baby Jack), baulked at that. 'Okay, let's calm down now, shall we?' She placed a comforting arm on Seb, who took a deep breath and relaxed a little.

'Maybe it's not such a big deal. If your parents do see each other today and they realize things don't quite add up, maybe they'll just think that you got it wrong. They won't question it.' She sounded a little uncertain of that, and after the morning inquisition we'd had just getting to the train station, I could understand why.

'Now, if we could all just focus for a second.' Seb and I looked at Bell. 'Are we doing this or not?'

'Of course we're doing this!' I said, determined. We were tantalisingly close to making this actually happen, to pulling this off and solving this mystery of how to fix everything. We couldn't give up now. *I* couldn't give up now.

Bell gave Seb a nudge. 'What do you say, Captain?'

Seb tugged on his earlobe, looking at the ground. He shrugged. 'I guess.'

'In that case, get your running shoes on, boys.' Bell rolled her shoulders and neck, stretching her arms for good measure.

'Huh? For what?'

'The train leaves in fourteen minutes,' Bell called over her shoulder, already haring down the street. 'Unless you want to walk all the way to London!'

Before we could take off after her, I grabbed Seb gently by the elbow.

'If you don't want to do this, we can cancel and go play arcade games for the day,' I said. 'If you want to.'

Seb shook his head immediately. 'You want to go. You need to go. And you can't go without me or you'll be caught before the train is out of the station.' We locked eyes for a second, unsaid promises being spoken silently between us. Seb nodded slightly and I grinned.

'Are you boys coming or what?!' Bell yelled from the corner.

We took off sprinting, hoping with all our might that Dad was our last unplanned obstacle of the day.

CHAPTER 20

I GUESS THERE'S NO TURNING BACK

'GO, GO, GO!' Bell yelled as the station suddenly came into view, looming in the distance.

All three of us were sweating, our hearts pounding out of our chests. A quick glance at my watch told me we had six minutes to make it into the station, through the ticket barriers and onto the 11:13 train. We were cutting it fine, even if everything was working in our favour.

We didn't stop as we neared the station entrance, careering through and around the crowds to get inside. We began pushing our way through, fighting through seas of elbows and bags, and leaping over lazily pulled luggage. When we got inside, the departure boards hovered above us. My eyes frantically moved from one screen to the next, again and again, but nothing made sense and time seemed to be ticking in my ears, reminding me that we had minutes left to get on board.

Seb was standing stock-still in the middle of a crowd of people jostling around him, staring intently at the screens. He nodded to himself after a couple of seconds.

'Platform eight,' he said over the din.

We moved with the flow of people towards the barriers. As soon as I saw them, I thanked my lucky stars. They were open! The first thing to actually go our way. Then I saw a man guarding the gates, a large and menacing-looking ticket machine strapped to his shoulder, and my excitement fizzled.

The man may as well have had 'mean' tattooed on his forehead. His eyes were narrowed as they inspected every single ticket, framed by thick eyebrows that were furrowed into a constant frown. Just one look told me that he hated children. He would be the type to puncture a football kicked into his garden rather than hand it back. He probably had a 'NO KIDS' sign nailed to his garden gate. One arm all but petted the ticket machine he was carrying, waiting like a lion to leap on his prey. In this case, that prey was anybody who had no right to be crossing the barriers, us included.

There wasn't any way to stop and come up with an idea to get around this obstacle. People were pressing in on us from all sides and all three of us were quickly separated in the rush. I wasn't so much walking forward as being carried in the direction of the platform. It was like riding a wave.

As the barriers neared, I did the only thing that sprang to mind and dipped my head low. I also bent my knees, trying to walk in time with a young couple who were holding hands in the hope that they would shield me from view. Out of the corner of my eye, I saw Seb do the same, ducking next to a rather large suitcase. I couldn't see Bell but hoped she wasn't far.

Almost too soon, the open ticket barriers were there and, just beyond, the platforms. We were going to make it! And then, just as I was ready to take a step into safety, a firm hand clamped down on my shoulder.

'Ticket, please,' a gruff voice spat.

I looked up, feeling the colour drain from my face. The ticket inspector towered over me, a grossly satisfied smirk toying with his mouth. I was almost surprised when he didn't lick his lips in anticipation of laying down the law on a twelve-year-old.

'Wh-what?' I said, frantically searching for Seb and Bell.

Seb was standing, horror-stricken, on the other side of the barriers. Bell was still nowhere to be seen.

'I said where's your ticket, lad? You can't be getting through here without one.'

I would love to say I began feigning idiocy, that I had willingly decided that playing dumb would be the best way forward. But that would be giving me too much credit. At that precise moment, my mouth was opening and closing like a fish out of water.

'Excuse me, sir?' I didn't recognize the voice. Or maybe I did, but it was like a dream that I couldn't quite recall. It was high and precise, over-enunciating each word like the person speaking them was savouring each one. When I whirled around and saw it was Bell, I nearly yelped in relief. But what was with the voice?

'What?' the ticket man said, almost snarling at the nerve to have been interrupted when he was going in for the kill.

'My name is Eliza Barclay Card ... The Fourth,' she added quickly. 'That's spelled IV, if you must know.' I started at that, confused. 'My father is a very important man, so I don't have time to dawdle, but I just thought you would like to know that there are a bunch of *boys*,' she said the word as if it disgusted her, 'over by the ticket machines, and they are writing absolutely *revolting* things on the screen with marker pens.'

The ticket man looked horrified at the prospect of his train station being vandalized. I couldn't help but notice that he also looked a little excited, probably because telling off a group of kids was better than telling off one.

'I hate to be vulgar, but I think they are even drawing a . . . well, you know . . .' Bell sniffed as if she were greatly offended. Without a second more hesitation, the ticket inspector bolted off through the crowd.

'God speed,' Bell called after him. Then she set her sights on me, her new voice suddenly gone and a sly grin on her face.

'Barclay Card the Fourth?' I uttered, still trying to wrap my head around this new name.

'I saw it on the front of a letter before I left my house this morning. I thought it sounded fancy. I told you, new identities will get us to London and back undetected! Now, go!' hissed Bell, pushing me through the barriers.

My legs finally remembered that they were not made of concrete and we propelled ourselves through the

open gates onto the platform. But there was no time for celebrations. We had a train to catch.

'It's platform eight!' Seb yelled over his shoulder, shooting for the stairs and taking them two at a time.

We weaved around suitcases with the elegance of elephants that needed glasses. As we reached the top of the stairs, I saw a train slowly grind to a halt alongside a platform with a glittering number eight painted on the wall.

'It's here!' I shouted, nearly tripping over a pushchair in my haste.

The three of us sped up, rounding the corner and thundering down the stairs until we hit the ground of platform eight. The last people had just trickled on board and no sooner had we faced the train, a threatening beep sounded from the doors.

'GO! GET ON!' I pushed us all forward.

Bell was the first one on the train, followed by a red-faced and spluttering Seb, his glasses clinging desperately to the end of his nose. I hopped on as the doors began to slide shut. My foot was barely inside when they hissed menacingly and settled with a click.

'That was a close one,' Bell said in between deep breaths.

'I wonder when—' But she was cut off as the train lurched forward and began to slowly crawl out of the station. We were on board, and there was no turning back now.

'I can't believe we're doing this,' Seb said, faint as a whisper, for the hundredth time as we sat down at an empty table in a quiet carriage.

'I can't believe we're doing this,' Bell echoed, trying not to squeal with excitement. 'I still think the trench coats would've worked better, but we did it!'

I settled into a seat by the window, watching as the station slipped by, and nervous threads tied knots in my stomach. We were *actually* doing it. We were inching closer to London by the second, where Pride waited for us. Our postcard-pretty town gave way to rolling fields, which were almost luminous under the late-morning sun. It was already promising to be a warm day, with no cloud in the sky as far as the eye could see.

There were only a dozen or so people in our carriage, all spread out down the aisle. There was an old woman, her grey hair piled into a bun atop her ahead, poring over a crossword book; a dark-haired, headphone-wearing teenager no more than five years older than us; two young girls, who were chatting at a million miles an hour and for some reason refused to take off their sunglasses even though we were now inside; two boys with their backs to us, one with neon green hair that reminded me of Dean, except his was blue; and a small group of people spread out over two tables, laughing carelessly together.

It was this group that intrigued me most. They were teenagers by my guess, but the kind of teenagers who are almost not teenagers any more. Not only were they the loudest, they were the brightest too. One had bubblegum-pink hair that haloed her face, while the boy next to her wore a shirt that I knew Dad would describe as 'loud'. The boy opposite him had sprinkled his beard with at least six different colours of glitter. The final one seemed quieter than the rest. His hair was a regular colour and he didn't have a beard for glitter to go in. In comparison to his friends, his clothes were pretty regular, just a white T-shirt that had a small rainbow heart on the pocket. He smiled a lot too. So much so, my cheeks and jaw ached just from looking at him.

'Tickets, please,' a daunting voice said behind me, dragging me out of my thoughts. *Not again.*

I spun in my seat and peered down the aisle to the end of the carriage, where a tired-looking woman had appeared.

She carried a similar machine to the barrier guard back at the station. Not good news. Not good news at all.

'Um, guys,' I said, my heart and hopes plummeting. 'We have a problem.'

'What?' said Seb, rattled with panic already.

He and Bell looked down the aisle where the woman was in the middle of inspecting the headphone-wearing teenager's ticket. She might've been tired, but she made sure to examine the ticket properly. I couldn't help but notice that she, like the guard back home, looked stern. I began to wonder if being mean was a requirement for this particular field of work.

'Well, that's it,' Seb stuttered. 'We're done for. Goodbye freedom, it was nice knowing you.'

'Quick, let's move,' Bell muttered, ignoring Seb and hopping into the aisle to scurry in the opposite direction.

'Move where?' I said, trying to push my own dread back down to where it'd come from.

'Just away from here. Maybe we can hide somewhere until she's gone.'

We tried not to run, to look like we belonged on this train as much as anybody else. But there's not many places to hide on a train, and we soon reached the end of the road.

'You have to be kidding me,' I said, staring at the 'no entry' sign on the door at the other end of the carriage. I gave it a nudge but it was locked. The woman had made it halfway up the aisle, looking more frightening by the second.

'Our Father, who art in heaven,' Seb began, making the sign of the cross and peace with our impending doom. She still hadn't noticed us yet, but it couldn't be long before we were caught.

'Archie? Is that you?'

I knew that voice. We all did. I flexed my fingers, checking that this wasn't actually a nightmare, but they wiggled back at me.

'What are you doing here?' a second voice said, also familiar.

I slowly turned my head, hoping with all my might that I was wrong. Oscar and Dean looked back at me, blank and baffled at the same time. There was no use in trying to hide now. We'd been well and truly caught.

CHAPTER 21

FAMILIAR FACES

'Hi, Oscar. Hi, Dean. Sorry, no time to explain!' Bell quickly jumped under their table, much to Oscar and Dean's confusion. They looked like they'd seen the Loch Ness Monster doing a cartwheel.

Seb couldn't even open his mouth to speak. He just sank to the floor as if he were fainting and disappeared under the table next to Bell. At this, Oscar and Dean snapped out of their trance. They peered under the table and then back at me for answers.

'Archie? What's going on?' Oscar said, frowning. He sounded like I do when faced with fractions or algebra, but now wasn't the time to beg for forgiveness. A sense of dread washed over me as I glanced back down the aisle and saw the ticket woman getting closer and closer. She was no more than five or six seats down, handing tickets back to the girl with pink hair. Any second now and she'd turn around to find me standing there, no ticket in my pocket and no reason to be aboard a train to London.

'I'll explain, I promise,' I said in a rush. 'Just ... please don't say anything.' Hoping that would do the trick, although not betting my piggy bank on it, I slipped under the table, huddling as far away as possible from the aisle just as a thick, clumpy boot appeared.

'Tickets, please,' the woman said above us, apparently none the wiser that there were three almost-teenagers hiding by her feet.

'Uhh, yeah, tickets,' Oscar said, fumbling in his pocket.

Bell tapped me on the shoulder, nearly making me jump out of my skin. She pointed past my head and towards Dean's seat, where his phone was balancing precariously on the edge and ready to drop at the slightest shift. If it hit the floor, we were done for. Steadily, although my hands were shaking somewhat, I grabbed it between my thumb and finger and gingerly put it in my pocket. I guess you could say that was a ... close call. Yes, I'm here all week.

It seemed to take an age, but finally, the ticket woman

grumbled something I couldn't quite hear, handed Oscar and Dean their tickets, and began shuffling back the way she'd come. We counted to thirty, then to sixty for good measure. If I could've packed my bags and moved in under that table, I would've. It seemed much more appealing than facing what surely waited for us above. But when we couldn't possibly stall any longer, the three of us popped our heads out into the open. The ticket woman was gone, but Oscar and Dean were very much still there, waiting for answers.

'Fancy seeing you here,' Bell said with fake cheer. 'I think we should be going, though.'

'Hey, not so fast!' Oscar sat up straight and inspected the three of us closely, Dean's narrow, pointed face hovering over his shoulder, his once-blue hair now the colour of luminous slime. If only I'd looked more closely at the green head I'd spotted when we first got on the train, then maybe we wouldn't be here, waiting for thunder and lightning to strike. Three seconds of silence was enough to crack us. Even I was disappointed that we didn't last longer.

'They made me do it!' Seb blurted, even though nobody had asked him anything yet.

'Traitor,' Bell muttered.

'Made you do what?' Dean looked even more suspicious than Oscar. He hovered off his seat, looking over our heads and down the carriage, his long fingers locked together tightly. 'Where are your parents?'

Oscar suddenly seemed to remember that parents were indeed what we were missing and peered down the aisle, expecting to see Mum or Dad on our tail. But, of course, they were nowhere in sight.

'Someone want to tell me what's going on?' Oscar raised his eyebrows expectantly, as if there must be a perfectly good reason why we were on a train to London with no parents. Seb had already landed us in the mud, and there wasn't any easy way to explain our way out of it, so there was nothing else to do other than come clean and hope for the best.

'We're on our way to London,' I said, sheepishly.

'Clearly,' Dean quipped back, unimpressed. His dark eyebrows knitted together some more as the three of us shrank back slightly. We didn't really know Dean at all, besides him being the star pupil who deserved his own statue, but everybody knew that. He was older than us and cooler than us which automatically made him terrifying. Even Bell seemed a little wary of him.

'But why? And where are your parents?' Oscar said again, craning his neck to look about the carriage once more and clearly expecting Mum or Dad to materialize out of thin air. Dean scrunched his eyebrows even closer together, studying the three of us carefully and ready to solve this unpleasant mystery that had landed under his nose.

'Oh, Oscar, please don't be mad at us. I promise we weren't going to cause any trouble or anything!' I squawked, sounding more like a chicken clucking with every word.

'What do I have to be mad about . . .?' Oscar trailed off and waited for me to pick up the slack.

I glanced at Bell and Seb out of the corner of my eye, searching for help. Bell hesitated, then gave a small, tight nod. Seb pulled his jacket up over his eyes. There was nothing else for it but to tell the truth, so I took a deep, shaky breath and started talking at a hundred miles an hour.

If we hadn't been about to get in the biggest trouble of our lives, watching Oscar and Dean's reaction might've been funny. First, they looked blank, although Dean still had a frown that was getting deeper by the second. I went a little around the houses in explaining, trying to dress up

our story so it wouldn't seem so bad. But it seemed there was no way to make what we'd done sound any less ... well, silly.

By the time I'd finished, Oscar looked like he might be sick. Dean didn't look much better, having recoiled into the window probably in the hope that it might give way and let him off the train. As for me, Bell and Seb, we all looked exactly how we should – like schoolkids that had been caught red-handed and knew that there was no getting out of it.

'We're turning back around IMMEDIATELY,' Dean spluttered, his green hair sticking up in tufts from where he'd raked his hands through it. He looked like he'd been electrocuted. 'The second we get into London, we're getting on the first train back home.'

I nodded, ashamed and trying not to burst into tears. It was all my fault we were here in the first place, and all my fault that we'd now been caught.

'It was my idea. At least don't tell their parents,' I pleaded desperately, pointing at Bell and Seb. I thought about how Seb's mum might react and, for a brief moment, it felt like I had stepped out of my body to float in the ether. The picture in my mind made me shiver just thinking about it. Even Bell's parents, who for the most part trusted her to figure things out for herself, would be disappointed by our adventure, and that was almost worse. Not quite, but almost.

'Hold on a minute, how about we all just take a breath for a second.' Oscar inhaled deeply to demonstrate, gesturing to the empty chairs on the other side of the table. The three of us squeezed into them.

'Now, I'll admit that what you've done is ... well, it's stupid, let's just say that.' Oscar grimaced. 'Getting on a train to London on your own without your parents, and without them even knowing, is dangerous at best. What if something happened to you while you were there and nobody knew where to look for you?'

I mean, it was obvious now that Oscar was saying it out loud how silly we'd been. Hearing our plan spoken back to us was really highlighting that with neon marker pens and underlining it for good measure.

'But ...' Oscar was clearly battling to find the right words. He glanced at Dean, who didn't look at all happy about the situation and had now folded his arms to make his point. Oscar shrugged. 'We can't send them back home.'

Dean sank into his chair a little more, clearly sulking. 'I'm not babysitting three kids in the middle of London. If we lose them, or something happens, then it's our fault just as much as theirs.'

'We won't lose them,' Oscar said confidently, a little bounce back in his voice. 'I've babysat them a hundred times and have yet to lose one. Isn't that right, Archie?'

I jumped at the sound of my name and nodded a little too enthusiastically. Dean threw me a glare and turned back to Oscar. 'This is meant to be *our* day out together.'

Oscar thought about this for a second, staring at the table like that could give him the answer. Dean huffed, sulky and mean-faced and not at all impressed by the idea of us tagging along. I had a feeling that, nine-and-a-half times out of ten, Oscar would've taken his boyfriend's side and sent us straight back home.

'Okay, so how about this?' Oscar said finally, folding his hands together in front of him like he was about to announce something of the utmost importance. He took a deep breath and said, 'We'll take you to Pride.' He levelled me with a look as he said it, winking so quickly that it might never have happened.

Bell whooped and cheered, dragging me and Seb into a tight group hug while Dean rolled his eyes. The day had already been threatened too many times before it had even really begun. Now with Oscar and Dean on our side, there was no way that we could fail. We weren't going to give up now.

'But there are some rules,' Oscar said loudly over our cheers. We quietened back down and waited warily. 'First of all, you stay close to us at all times. The second one of you even thinks about getting more than a *millimetre* away, we're turning this ship around and sailing straight back home.'

We nodded in unison.

'Two: we're not staying for long. We'll show you the parade and then we're getting the hell out of dodge. Dean's right – we can't afford to lose you and the longer we stay, the more chance there is of that happening.'

Dean flinched at the thought but Oscar powered on. 'And we need a meeting point. Should the worst happen, God forbid, we need a place where we can find each other again. Somewhere that's big and easy to find and close to where we're going to be. You must've already had a meeting place in mind, right?'

The three of us looked blankly back at Oscar. He sighed so deeply, I wondered how he could have that much air in his lungs.

'How about that big archway between Buckingham Palace and Trafalgar Square?' Dean offered, still not entirely warming to Oscar's idea but at least thawing. He dug in his pocket, producing the flyer that we now knew all too well. This one wasn't ripped and faded, though. It looked shiny and brand new.

'Right there.' Dean pointed on the map, jabbing his finger down next to the cartoon drawing of the lions in Trafalgar Square. 'It's not labelled on the map, but you can't miss it. It's giant. And anyway, we're not going to *need* to use the archway because we're not going to lose each other, are we?' Dean said pointedly.

'That we're not. But, before I forget, there's one last thing.' Oscar began rooting around in his bag, rustling the contents until he found what he was looking for. 'If we're going to Pride, then you're going to look the part too. No black clothes allowed,' he said, looking us up and down. I didn't dare tell Oscar that we thought we'd be pretty much invisible if we wore dark clothing. Judging on how many times we'd been caught today, it clearly hadn't worked.

'Dig in, boys and girls,' Oscar said grandly, emptying a bag of what looked like half the beauty aisle of Boots.

Seb gingerly picked up a can of multicoloured hairspray like it was a stink bomb ready to explode at any second. 'What is it?' he said.

'May I?' Dean said, leaning forward and taking the can from a confused Seb's hand. He shook the bottle, a mischievous smirk flitting from one side of his mouth to the other. He was trying not to laugh and I was suddenly suspicious.

'You might wanna close your eyes,' he said, uncapping the bottle. 'All three of you, actually. Eyes shut for a moment, if you please.' Seb looked at me. I looked at Bell. Bell looked at the bottle and shrugged.

'What's the worst that can happen?' Bell said and scrunched her eyes tightly shut. Against our better judgement, me and Seb did the same.

There was a hiss, followed by a gasp that sounded like it came from Oscar. 'So cool,' he said under his breath. 'Where did you find this stuff?'

I felt Seb jump a little as the hiss sounded again, this time a little closer. He squirmed into me but I kept my eyes shut, not sure I wanted to see what was happening.

Then the hiss came again, this time directly in front of my face. A mist washed over my hair and forehead, cold and startling.

'Perfect,' Dean said, satisfied. 'You can open your eyes now.'

I opened one eye cautiously. I still had my sight, so that was something. Dean was grinning in earnest now, and Oscar was too. What had they done?

'Oh my God!' Seb said in my ear, louder than he needed to considering he was basically sitting in my lap. 'Your hair!' The frown fell away from my face the moment I saw Seb, whose own hair was glittering in the light from the sun seeping through the window. When he moved his head closer to get a better look at me, it shimmered red, then purple, then blue, then green.

Bell's hair was even more magnificent. She was eyeballing the loose strands in wonder, twiddling them in the sun rays and watching them glitter with all the colours of the rainbow.

'Pretty cool, huh? Although you'll be finding glitter in every nook and cranny until Halloween,' Oscar snorted. 'Take a look. Much better if you ask me.' He passed over a small pocket mirror and the three of us crowded around it. My hair looked normal at first glance. But, sure enough, the second I moved my head, the colours began to dance. If I held my head in just the right position, I looked like I was wearing the rainbow as a funny little hat.

'Does it ... come out?' Seb said cautiously, running a hand through his hair and looking at the glitter now in his palm.

'Yep. One wash and it's like it never happened.' Oscar side-eyed Dean, who shrugged. 'Okay, maybe two washes.'

Before we could dive into the rest of Oscar's weird and wonderful supplies, I felt my phone begin to vibrate. My heart stopped and started and stopped all over again as I slipped it out of my pocket and saw three letters on the screen.

'Hi, Dad,' I said after a pause, almost forgetting that it was pretty rude to answer the phone and not actually say anything. Seb clutched the table, his knuckles turning white as he took quick, shallow breaths. Oscar and Dean shared a nervous glance.

'Hi, Arch,' Dad said. He sounded far away, like he was holding the phone away from his mouth.

'What's up ...?' I said cautiously, trying not to sound too guilty. I was already wary of a trap. Did Dad know we were on the train and was trying to catch me out on a lie?

'Nothing! Do I need a reason to call my only son?' I laughed nervously but didn't answer, refusing to move in case I accidentally set off a hidden booby-trap.

'Just wanted to see how you're doing, that's all. We didn't get to talk properly before and we haven't had a proper catch-up in a while. Not since the arcade . . .' He trailed off.

I turned my back slightly on the others, who were all watching me like a hawk. 'I'm okay, how're you?'

'Nothing new to report. Same old, same old.' There was a pause, the line crackling softly in my ear. 'Hey, I thought maybe when I'm back we could hit up the arcade again, like old times. Get one of those ridiculous ice-cream sundaes we can never quite finish.'

'Sure.' I nodded into the phone. 'Where are you anyway?' I said it as casually as I could but my tone still flicked its tail with a wobble at the end. With a shiver, I quickly glanced over my shoulder to make sure Dad wasn't actually there.

Another pause. Then, 'Just at work. There are some bits and bobs I've got to get done. Apparently they can't wait until Monday. Sod's law! Anyway, I better get off. Just thought I'd call and say I love you. That's all.' We said our stilted goodbyes and hung up the phone. Maybe I hadn't been caught after all.

'So?' Bell said before I could even tuck the phone back in my pocket. My heartbeat wasn't even back to normal yet.

I (unsuccessfully) tried to shrug it off. 'It was nothing, no big deal. How far are we from London anyway?'

Bell narrowed her eyes so they were almost slits. Oscar studied me closely for a brief second but seemed to get the point. 'I think we're almost there,' he said, pointing at something in the distance.

And sure enough, the city loomed on the horizon, daunting and promising all at the same time.

CHAPTER 22

THIS WASN'T PART OF THE PLAN

'STAY CLOSE!!!!' Oscar yelled as we all piled off the train and were immediately swept up into the surging crowd. 'NO WANDERING OFF! I MEAN IT!'

It felt like our small town could've fit entirely in that London station, and with room to spare too. The vaulted ceilings curved high above us, patches of blue sky shining in through the windows as passengers spilled out onto the platforms. The particles of dust floating in the air may as well have been orbs of magic, casting a spell of majesty around our heads. My brain was fuzzy trying to take it all in, overwhelmed by how much my eyes could suddenly see.

We're finally here.

For the first time, I could hear Oscar panicking. Dean

was shuffling quickly along beside him, popping up on his tiptoes every couple of seconds in an attempt to keep us in view. The crowds of people were relentless, though, and it wasn't long until I could only see the green of Dean's head, bobbing like a buoy out at sea. But, as long as I could see that, everything would be fine, and the chance of losing somebody with neon green hair seemed slim.

Bell excitedly linked one arm through mine and the other through Seb's, forming a human chain that couldn't be broken. We clutched at each other, letting ourselves be carried with the crowd and swept out into the street, gazing about us in wonder. Between the train and the exit, which was no real distance at all, we saw all kinds of things that you'd never see back home:

1. A clown handing out flyers, one of which Bell grabbed with glee, tucking it into her pocket like a valuable trinket.

2. A rainbow walkway that stretched from the platform to the station exit and beyond.

3. A man who seemed rather jolly and was twirling a rainbow-coloured umbrella like it was a cheerleading baton.

4. A band of glitter-painted dancers moving around a small stereo speaker. They'd attracted a large crowd, who were chanting and whooping with delight. At one point, a dancer jumped down into the splits and the crowd went nuts.

5. A man, who mostly stood out because he appeared to be the only one in a mile's radius who wasn't smeared in rainbows, releasing giant bubbles the size of small cars that floated over our heads and up to the clouds.

6. Small groups of teenagers dotted around the station floor, eagerly painting each other's faces with make-up of every colour.

7. A unicorn trotting along by the road, tossing its mane from side to side and neighing like a horse.

8. Okay, that last one was a lie, but I wouldn't have been surprised.

We definitely weren't at home any more. Even the sunlight seemed more ferocious in London, glinting off every shiny surface and bathing everything in melted gold.

'We made it,' Bell breathed, wide-eyed with excitement as our adventure sprang up before us. We pushed our way out into a small corner of open space, breathing a little harder than usual from the thrill of finally being in London, thirstily drinking it all in.

'Uh, guys?' Seb said, stuttering slightly.

'Oh, look!' Bell said, pointing with excitement at the exit we'd just come from. A parade of colour streamed through it with no signs of slowing down, people waving more rainbow flags than I could count excitedly over their heads.

'Guys?' Seb breathed again, this time tugging on the hem of my T-shirt.

'They're so adorable!' Bell squealed as two identical toddlers waddled out of the scrum, their parents cooing and laughing, hands haloing the air around them in case they fell. Both toddlers were sucking on rainbow dummies, spit splattering their bibs that proudly announced: 'I love my dads'. I didn't see what was so adorable myself, but the adults around them were all thrilled by this feat of simply walking.

'Guys, t-t-TEN!' Seb blurted. Hearing our emergency code, not to mention the panic in Seb's voice, immediately set my hairs on end. His brow was furrowed in on itself, worry lines crinkling his forehead like crumpled paper.

'Ten?' Bell said absently, watching as the toddlers and their dads posed for a photo next to a rainbow-coloured archway made up of balloons.

'What is it?' I said, as Seb looked around manically. For a moment, he looked like one of those bobble-headed dogs, his eyes bouncing from one place to another without a second's rest.

'They've gone?' It sounded like a question, as if he couldn't quite believe what his mouth was saying and his eyes were seeing.

And that's when I realized it too.

'What is it?' Bell said, all business and concern. Then, like a bad cartoon, the hammer dropped. 'Oh my God. Where are they?'

I jumped up onto the bench with more speed than I thought I was capable of, peering over the heads of the people swarming around us. Even more people were arriving now, spilling out of the station without an end in sight. Oscar and Dean were nowhere to be seen. I frantically searched from my vantage point, Bell and Seb standing up to join me. But the more I looked, the less I could see. It was like every single one of the moving heads – and there had to be hundreds – were blurring into one. Finding Dean in a crowd back at home would be easy – you just had to look for the only patch of neon-coloured hair. But here in London was different. There was pink hair and red hair, purple and blue. I spotted a slick of green in the crowd and my entire body sighed with relief. But, in almost comical slow-motion, the person turned around and I realized it wasn't Dean at all.

'Okay, let's bring this back down to a five,' I said, trying to ignore the tremor in my voice. 'We'll just call them. They can't be far away, right?' I dug out my phone and found Oscar's number but it didn't even ring.

'Try Dean,' Bell said, trying to remain calm and in control of the quickly spiralling situation. With shaking hands, I found Dean's number and pressed the phone to my ear. It rang once and there was silence. Then, with a tinkle of exhilaration, we all heard the blissful notes of a ringtone, almost calling us to safety.

'I told you they couldn't be far,' I said excitedly,

whipping my head around, almost certain Dean would be standing right there. But he was nowhere to be seen.

'Uh, Archie?' Seb said nervously, and he pointed to my pocket. With mounting dread, I fished out Dean's phone. Of course – I'd picked it up on the train to stop it from falling to the ground while the inspector checked their tickets. The phone screen was now lit up in my hand, my own name flashing tauntingly back at me. A lurch of panic ricocheted through my body.

'Well,' Bell said bluntly, blowing out her cheeks. 'I hate to say it, boys, but I think we might be lost.' She glanced at Seb and quickly tried to make amends. 'But I still don't think this can be any higher than a six. A seven at the very worst.'

As quick as our adventure had begun, it had disintegrated right in front of us, like paper burned to ash and floating away on the breeze. Now we were lost in a city so big, you could probably fly to the moon quicker than get to the other side of it.

Seb whimpered something that sounded suspiciously like the number twelve on our panic code. I didn't need to look at his face to see the obvious. He was terrified and didn't care who knew it. He slid behind me slightly, screwing up his eyes and opening them drastically, like if he did it fast enough, he might wake up from this terrible dream.

I pulled my rucksack from my back and started ripping through it, looking for something, anything, to help us. I held up my swimming trunks lamely.

'Yes, that will be a terrific help,' Bell said bluntly.

I ignored her and stuffed them back where they'd come from. Apart from that, there was nothing but a bottle of water and a banana. Unless the fruit was about to reveal itself as Oscar in disguise, there was nothing here that was going to help. Defeated, I went to zip up the bag, but then I spotted something I'd packed last minute, nestled against the lining. It was the picture of me and Dad. I doubted it would be much help, but I made a wish on it anyway. I would've done anything to get our day back on track.

'Well, we can't just stay here,' Bell said, finally tired of watching me hop from one foot to the other while swearing that Oscar and Dean must be close by. Then she dropped her voice to a low rumble. 'Don't look up now or do anything dramatic, but we're being watched.'

I immediately spun on the spot, peering with little subtlety at the train station exit. Bell tutted behind me but I didn't care because now I'd seen it too. Two people, a man and a woman with official-looking badges, were standing against the wall, muttering to each other while frowning in our direction. Every couple of seconds, they would sweep their eyes across the crowd before bringing them back to rest on us. And it wasn't like we were hard to miss, standing on a bench a good head and shoulders above everybody else.

'Maybe they're just train drivers?' I shrugged, although even I didn't believe that.

'Or maybe it's the undercover police waiting to take us to prison!' Seb squawked. 'Carly said she saw undercover police once and they looked just like that, I swear!' Seb drank in another eyeful. 'They're probably MI6. They once interviewed Carly about a top-secret mission, but she couldn't accept because we had a Biology exam that week. They're here to take us away! We've been caught!'

'Or *maybe* they're just station staff and we should think about moving,' Bell hissed, a smile on her face as if she were telling me about the weather. 'Nothing too sudden. Just start walking an—'

Seb didn't need to be told twice, although he seemed not to have listened to the instruction properly. Instead of casually walking away like we were all meant to be there, he jumped down from the bench and bounded off up the street, his arms flailing helplessly by his side. Bell and I saw the man and the woman start, unsure of what to do but coming towards us all the same.

'Run!' I yelled, and hot-footed it after Seb, who was already halfway down the street.

We didn't stop running, rounding one corner and then another, taking a right and then a left and then another left with no real direction or thought of where we were heading. Only when I had a stitch did I call for us to stop, but who knows how long we had been running by then.

'Do you think we lost them?' Seb spluttered, bent in two with his hands on his knees, huffing and puffing with concerning force, his glasses askew.

'Think so,' I said, looking around to check that the coast was clear before collapsing into an ungraceful heap on the pavement. I put my head between my knees and tried my hardest not to be sick. This day was already going from bad to worse and I didn't want it to continue with vomit down my T-shirt.

'Well . . . now what?' Seb looked at Bell, Bell looked at me, I looked at Seb. Our faces all mirrored each other, blank as paper with just a little fear and panic added in for good measure.

Bell stood up straight, taking a deep breath and smoothing her hair back. It was still glistening with the spray we'd used on the train a lifetime ago. 'Okay, let's think about this properly,' she said. She thought for a second but came up blank. 'I have no ideas. Anybody else?'

'Those books were a great help,' Seb grimaced, his face still flushed. Bell muttered something about trench coats under her breath. 'Options,' he said, slightly short of breath. 'One, we go back to the station and hope we find Oscar and Dean. They're probably still looking for us. But those people might still be there, and they'll definitely phone our parents.'

The sweat on my back turned cold. That idea didn't sound great, and we'd already failed at finding Oscar and Dean by staying close to the station. 'What else have we got?'

Seb shrugged. 'We just go home?' There was hope in his voice, soft and tentative, like the idea might scarper away from us now it was out in the open. 'It'd be easy to get back into the station, and once we're home, we can't get

into any more trouble.'

I felt myself deflate. We'd been so close to Pride, to figuring out the answers that would bridge the void between me and Dad. And we'd overcome so much just to get here in the first place. But if our adventure was a video game, our final life was blinking in danger on the screen. We were coming to the end.

But Bell shook her head firmly and an ember of hope appeared. 'When Oscar and Dean don't find us here, they'll do something dramatic, like call the police and announce that they've lost three kids in the middle of London,' she said. 'You know what Oscar's like. He won't risk going back home without us.'

'Is there an option three?' I asked, my mouth dry.

Seb dropped his gaze, suddenly finding interest in his shoelaces.

'Of course there is,' Bell said brightly. 'We go on.' Seb groaned but she ignored him and carried on. 'We came here to do one thing and that was go to Pride. There's no use in us standing by the train station and hoping Oscar and Dean will find us. We have to go and find them. They know where we were heading.' Bell suddenly stopped in her tracks, her face lighting up like sunrise. 'The archway!'

221

she squealed.

Seb looked confused but I understood straight away. 'Trafalgar Square!' I thought hard for a minute, trying to remember. 'Oscar said if we got lost, all we had to do was wait underneath the archway next to Trafalgar Square. He told us we couldn't miss it because it's right next to Buckingham Palace!'

'Does anybody know how to read a map?' Bell said, digging around in her bag for her phone. 'Surely we can figure this out.'

Bell dropped down next to me and the three of us crowded around the screen while all around us, London continued to blare its horn. The map stared menacingly back at us, refusing to yield an answer to this mess without a challenge. A little blue dot pulsed in the centre – it took me an embarrassingly long time to realize this dot was actually us – with a tiny arrow facing towards the road opposite. The blue dot looked like a fly trapped in a spider web of roads, which wasn't exactly great news for us.

Bell tilted the phone one way and the little arrow moved with it, swivelling to face the road next to us. She tilted it back, then turned it some more until she'd completed a full circle and the arrow was back facing the way it had started.

'Helpful,' I chirped.

Bell glowered in my direction.

'Oh, give it here,' Seb tutted. He grabbed the phone and brought it close to his face, like that was going to solve the mystery. He swiped one way, then the other, pinched the screen for one second before spreading his fingers across it the next.

'Here,' he said finally, hovering his finger over the map. Bell and I peered over his shoulder. The blue dot was nowhere to be seen but Seb looked mildly triumphant.

'Uhhhh?' said Bell, uncertain. 'Where are we looking, Sebastian?'

Seb rolled his eyes. He zoomed in on the map and flipped the phone around to face us. 'This is where we're meant to be. That's where the archway is.'

'Right,' I said, still not sure exactly where Seb was pointing. 'And where are we now?'

Seb pinched the screen once more, zooming out until the blue dot appeared in the corner of the screen. 'We're here.'

'And we need to get all the way over there?' Bell traced her finger from the blue dot and through a cluster of streets. 'Looks far, Seb. We could get the bus?'

Seb shook his head so quickly, I thought it might fall off. 'Adults everywhere. Three twelve-year-olds on their own is bound to draw attention. And Mum said buses aren't safe because they don't have seat belts so we should avoid them at all costs.'

'We walk then,' I said, pointing to the map again to drag Seb away from reciting any more from his *Mum Said This Is Dangerous* folder. That file had a *lot* of material. 'It says it's just over a mile. It can't take *that* long.' I hopped up onto my feet, a newfound spring in my step.

'Or we could always go back,' said Seb hopefully. 'Give it a couple of minutes for that crowd to disappear and then hop back on the train?'

Bell gave him a playful nudge, grinning mischievously. 'And where would the fun be in that?' She suddenly leaped up, standing over us with excitement rolling off her in waves. 'We never get the chance to have an adventure. This is our time! We're almost teenagers and it's time we started acting like it. This could be a day that we remember for the rest of our lives. Let's pull ourselves together and have the adventure we were meant to have in the first place, before Oscar and Dean butted in. Let's do this!' She finished, triumphant in all her glory.

'An adventure? Sounds like another word for trouble to me.' Trust Seb to pour cold water over Bell's inspirational speech. He sighed heavily, like the world had sprouted legs and jumped onto his shoulders with glee.

'Archie?' He looked at me imploringly, eyes big and pleading.

I thought about going home. I really did. But I also couldn't help thinking that we had almost made it. Yes, we had lost Oscar and Dean, but we were so close to where we were meant to be. There was this irresistible force that was pulling me closer, pushing me onwards; this small but insistent voice like an echo inside my ear telling me that it would all be worth it if only we just kept going.

'Oscar said to meet him under the archway. We'll be fine, Seb, I promise!' I wasn't sure I even believed my own comforting words, but I wasn't about to let Seb know that. 'We just follow the map, find Oscar and Dean, and then we can get home with no problems.' Seb groaned while Bell did a mini victory jig.

'That's settled, then,' she said. 'Let's get going before

something else goes wrong.'

'If things go bad, we can always come back,' I said to Seb, trying to nudge him reassuringly. 'Honestly, we can do this. We're almost there.'

'Okay,' he finally murmured. 'But if we get caught, I'm saying you forced me here against my will and wouldn't let me go back home.'

'Fine with me,' Bell sang, and she began marching off down the street.

'Wrong way,' Seb sighed. Bell sidled back and began in the other direction, whistling to herself. 'We're doomed,' said Seb. 'So freakin' doomed.'

CHAPTER 23

YOU'VE GOT TO BE KIDDING ME

So, there we were, the three of us marching through the streets of London on our way to Pride. Except we weren't really marching – Seb was mooching, dragging his feet and eyeing up potential dangers (aka everything), I was shuffling, my excitement shaded with nerves and anticipation, and Bell was skipping in the middle like this was the best day out we'd ever had.

London is an odd place, I have to admit. Captain Obvious would point out that it's just so *big*. Everything looks like it's been crammed into a machine invented by an evil genius and enlarged to cartoonish proportions. There is nothing small about London at all. But there's also a buzz that lingers over every street, lurking around every corner. It's thick in the air and warms you like a coat in winter, the thrill of the city pulling you in every time. I haven't been to many places in the world, but I'm sure there's nowhere quite like it.

Aside from one diversion (the street we were *meant* to go down was overrun with police vans and flashing lights that had Seb nearly passing out, so we'd chosen to go the long way around), everything was, dare I say it, going just fine. The road was as straight as a ruler, bookmarked at the end by the London Eye, which watched us loyally from the horizon as we got closer.

And that buzz in the air only got more palpable, thumping through our bodies like a bass guitar. Snatches of laughter surfed over our heads, echoed by hoots of joy. Rainbow flags peeked out at us from everywhere, winking with the promise that this scattered trail of multicoloured breadcrumbs would take us to where we needed to be. Pride was close. I could feel it.

'What do you think this whole thing is going to be like?' I mused as we slipped behind two girls who'd fused themselves together under one large pink, white and blue flag. I made a mental note to Google what that stood for later.

'Like one big party?' Bell couldn't hide her thinly veiled wonder as someone stopped in the middle of the road to do a cartwheel. As if to mark her point, a bunch of friends linked arms and set off a chorus of party poppers.

'Actually, it's meant to be a protest,' Seb said matter-of-factly. 'Honestly, did either of you read up about any of this before we came?'

'We knew you would be the one to read all about it and tell us everything,' said Bell. 'Wait a minute, is that what this is all about?' She slipped a hand into her pocket, retrieving the flyer that the clown had given her at the station. She underlined the title with her finger: PRIDE IS STILL A PROTEST!

'See, I told you,' Seb said, pushing his glasses up his nose and trying to get a better look at the flyer. We couldn't read and walk at the same time, so we ducked out of the Pride wave and huddled close together.

'Pride is still a protest,' Seb read. 'While the rights of the LGBT+ community ha—'

'The Elle Betty who?' Bell frowned.

'LGBT,' Seb corrected while Bell typed it into her phone and hit search.

I leaned in for a closer look, shielding the screen from the view of passers-by – I might not agree with everything Sabine tells us, but she'd been pretty convincing about guarding your pockets from thieves in a city like London.

'Lesbian, gay, bicycle—' I said, trying to read Bell's phone from an angle close to upside down.

Seb shook his head. 'Lesbian, gay, *bisexual* and *transgender*.' In my defence, he was looking at the phone the right way up.

'I'm still not following,' Bell said, scrunching up her face to try and make better sense of it all.

'Well, it's obvious, isn't it?' I said, determined to correct my reading blunder but actually not sure it was entirely obvious at all. I raised four fingers. 'Lesbian: a girl who likes girls.' I dropped one. 'Gay: a boy who likes boys.' I dropped another, then risked a glance at Seb to make sure I was right. 'Bisexual . . .' I petered out.

'Someone who likes more than one,' Bell butted in. 'I know that.'

'How?' said Seb.

'Bi means two, dummy. Ever heard of a bicycle?'

'What about the fourth one?' I said, trying to keep the focus.

'Transgender – someone who feels like they've been born into the wrong body,' Seb said, matter-of-factly. 'Oh, and while I was looking it up, there's sometimes a plus on the end. Like, the symbol plus?'

'We're doing maths now?' I choked, horrified.

Seb rolled his eyes. 'I think the plus is for everybody else who is a part of the community. That's what it said on Google anyway. LGBT+,' he finished with a flourish.

'How is it that you know everything?' Bell moaned.

'Maybe you should try reading *helpful* books for once.' Seb smirked, hopping away from Bell as she aimed a kick at his shins.

'And what does the rest of it say.' I pointed to the flyer still in Bell's hand. She smoothed it back out and we began to read once more.

PRIDE
IS STILL A PROTEST!

While the rights of the LGBT+
community have undoubtedly leaped
forward over the years, we cannot
forget those who are still left fighting
for basic human rights; rights that
most of us take for granted.

Pride began as a protest on the streets of New York City.
Now, more than half a century later, we are able to gather
every year and celebrate our colourful community, but we
mustn't forget that the fight still continues.

We mustn't leave any part of our community behind.

'You never completely have
your rights, one person, until
you all have your rights.'
Marsha P. Johnson

'So, it's not a party?' Bell asked carefully, still reading
parts of the flyer. 'Interesting. It sounds like ... I don't

know, like it means something . . .'

'Something *more*,' I finished, as a passing woman hugged a rainbow flag tightly around herself. The pieces of the Pride puzzle, of the buzz that danced in the air all around us, were starting to fall into place. You could see in the faces of the crowd, in the joy and pride and pure elation. Of *course* it meant much more. You just had to look at the three of us, in the middle of London and searching for answers, to see that.

'Where are we anyway?' Bell traded the flyer for her phone, inspecting the map and checking that we were still on course.

'I don't *think* we're too far away. I don't understand this thing at all.' She cupped the screen with one hand against the glare of the beating sun. 'Oh, I give up. Seb, you loo—'

'DUCK!' Seb suddenly shrieked, yanking us both behind a bright red phone box. The immediate crowd around us jumped half out of their skins, tutting and frowning as Seb cowered between us. His face had gone so pale, I thought he might turn to ash or smoke and float off up into the clouds.

'Seb, what on *Earth* is wrong with you,' Bell started, but Seb held up his hand and motioned for us all to get lower.

That feeling of ice seeping through my body set my heart on high alert. What now?

'Look,' Seb whispered, pointing a shaking finger across the street. 'It's your dad.'

I laughed, because what would my dad be doing in London when he'd just told me on the phone that he was actually at work?

'Don't be silly, it's probably just someone that looks like him is all,' I said confidently.

But when the three of us peeped out from behind the phone box and searched across the street, sure enough, there was my dad. I gasped and jumped backwards into Bell, who stifled a yelp as I trod on her foot. He hadn't seen us yet, but he seemed to be deep in thought, motionless as if he'd been struck by a sudden Eureka moment. People slipped and pushed past him, an immovable rock in the middle of a chaotic stream.

'What's he doing here?' Bell muttered, tired of surprises trying to ruin her great adventure. 'Did you know he was coming today?'

I shook my head, my insides feeling like writhing snakes. We watched as Dad dug out his phone and tapped intensely for a minute. Then, pocketing it once more, he was off, striding down the street in the direction we'd been heading with sudden purpose.

And I was off too. I don't know what came over me, or what pushed me to leap out from behind the phone box and start running after him. I guess I wanted to know where he was going or what he was doing, although at this point I had a vague idea. I just wanted to know if I was right. I didn't know what I would do when I caught up with him, or how I would explain our situation if he spotted the three of us in London. But that's the thing about impulse – it rarely relies on reason or logic, and we already know I don't have much of either.

'Archie! Where are you going?! Come back!' Bell yelped, but her voice was snatched away by the revving of an impatient taxi.

I swerved and weaved my way through the crowd, which only got thicker and more impenetrable, not to mention increasingly colourful and chaotic, the further down the street I got. I could still see Dad, just up ahead and across the road, but I was starting to lose him. Then, because the stars never quite align how you want them to, I jumped around a man and his dog, only to collide with a middle-aged couple and their dozens of shopping bags.

The collision was spectacular. Half the contents of the bags erupted up into the air, seemingly in slow motion. A brand-new floral dress floated back down to drape itself over the man's head, while a can of what appeared to be tuna rolled off down the street as if it were in a hurry to get somewhere else.

'I'm s-s-so so s-sorry,' I stuttered, half out of fear and half out of breath. Bell suddenly appeared, can of tuna in hand. She smiled sweetly and offered it back to the woman, who was still clearly in shock.

'Eliza Barclay Card the Fourth,' she said, elongating her words once more so they were impossibly long. 'Sorry about him, he doesn't get out much.' Bell gave me a stern side-eye. 'Lovely dress, by the way! It really suits you, sir! Shall we?' The couple gawped at us, but before they could say anything, Bell began pulling me down the street.

'I repeat,' Bell said when we were a safe distance away. 'What the hell?! Are you trying to get us killed?'

'Where did he go?' I said, whirling on the spot like a ballerina, although admittedly less graceful. I couldn't see Dad anywhere.

'He was right behind me,' Bell said absently, also spinning around on the spot. 'Seb?'

'I wasn't talking about Se—' I trailed off, swallowing the rest of the sentence. 'Wait, where's Seb?'

'You have *got* to be kidding me,' Bell breathed in disbelief.

The crowd penned us in on all sides, ever-moving and unyielding. But Seb, he was nowhere to be seen.

CHAPTER 24

SEE A PENNY, PICK IT UP

And so, the day was only getting worse. Except now things had really hit rock bottom. I couldn't quite believe that Seb might be lost, somewhere in this gigantic city on his own. I thought about how quick he was to panic about the slightest thing going wrong and my heart seemed to stop and start all at the same time. At last year's nativity play, Seb accidentally shone his spotlight on the three wise jocks instead of Jesus (who was called Jessica in our version and went to Bethlehem High). He still shuddered thinking about it. Now, here he was, lost in London.

This wasn't good. This wasn't good at all.

'This can't be happening,' said Bell, echoing my thoughts. 'Seb! Get out here immediately! This is not funny! If this is your idea of a joke I will personally . . .' I shouldn't repeat the rest of that sentence. I think even Bell would be surprised to read that back.

But Seb didn't appear. Other than frowns and tuts from people trying to get by, we were truly on our own with no Seb in sight.

'How is it possible to lose *three* people in one day? In not even an *hour*!' Bell ran a hand through her hair and squeezed her eyes tight shut. 'I guess this is a ten after all.'

I tried to speak, to say something, anything, that might solve this nightmare. But my voice had snagged in my throat and vanished altogether. Everything seemed closer than before, pressing in on us from all sides. It felt like I couldn't breathe, like if I even tried I might just break into little pieces. I thought about this morning, about the last few weeks, about how everything had mounted up until now, when it was all about to tip and come crashing back down. And I thought about Dad – how he'd lied to me on the phone about being at work, how he'd seemingly lied or kept things from me for a while now. We'd never been like that before. My fury was only trumped by my sadness, which watered down every emotion I had left.

And so I burst into tears. Not silent tears either. I mean

a full-body convulsion, that feral-sounding sob that claws its way up from somewhere deep inside.

Bell didn't pause for a second. She wrapped me up in a hug, her arms circling around my head and protecting me from the inquisitive looks of passers-by. She gently steered me towards a quieter corner and let me cry it out. It took a minute or three.

'I think it makes a cool new accessory,' Bell said, looking at a glob of snot I'd left on the front of her T-shirt. We both laughed, although mine was shaky from the tears. 'So, I guess we need a new pla—'

'Excuse me? Is everything all right?' We both froze, neither of us turning around, in the hope that the voice wasn't for our ears. But when we didn't move a muscle, it came again. 'Hello? Do you need help or something?'

We both turned around slowly. I don't know about Bell, but I was expecting to see the police, or at least the security guards from back at the station. But when we saw who the voice belonged to, Bell gasped, although she stifled it pretty well with a cough. My jaw hit the floor so hard, I was surprised that I didn't hear a cartoonish *CLANG!* to go with it.

Two people looked back at us, concern etched on their

faces. But their faces didn't look like yours or mine, or even Mum's when she's really dolled herself up for a night at the bingo. Their faces were like art canvases, other-worldly in their colour and perfection. A sweeping brush stroke blushed their cheeks, reaching up to their hair, which was covered in a cap made of tape. Their eyelids were various shades of the rainbow, one colour seeping into the next.

They saw us staring, open-mouthed and unmoving. The taller of the two, pale and fair even with the make-up, laughed a pleasant tinkle that sounded like music. 'Oh, don't worry about all of this. It comes off after a shower or two.'

The smaller one chuckled too, fuller and deeper. He reminded me a little of my grandad, his dark skin immaculate in the beaming sun. Unlike my grandad, however, he was wearing purple lipstick. His voice alone took up more room than the first, like he was in charge. His blushed cheeks looked like they were filled with more laughter. 'Christ, we must look like psychopaths,' he said.

'Beautiful psychopaths, though, don't ya think?' The first one framed his face with his hands, looking up towards the clear blue sky and posing for the sun.

The shorter one waved him off with a flick of his hand. 'All right, Linda Evangelista, knock it off.' He stuck his hand out into the space between us. 'I'm Divine Sublime.' He leaned in closer, as if he were about to reveal a huge secret. 'But my real name's Lester,' he said with a grin. 'It's nice to meet you.'

'And I'm Penny—'

'MICHAEL!' Lester dropped his head into his hands. 'They're *kids*. How about you just give them your *real* name.'

'Oh, yeah. Uh, I'm Michael. Nice to meet ya.' Both of their hands lingered in front of us expectantly. Bell, of course, took the plunge first, warily shaking their hands. I followed suit, offering the hand that hadn't been plagued with my own tears and snot.

'Sooooo ...' Lester tried again. 'Everything okay over here? Sorry to butt in but we could hear you crying from halfway down the street. Sounded like an emergency, and I'd hate to leave a sister in need.' Michael nodded along, Lester clearly the more confident leader. He was basically our Bell.

Seb's warning about letting adults into our plan echoed in my ears, although that just made me tear up again as I remembered he still wasn't here and was instead lost and alone somewhere in the city. Bell gave me a searching look, her brain doing double-time to figure out what we should do next. For once, though, I took the lead. Not having adults in on our plan from the start clearly hadn't worked so far. What was the worst that could happen now?

'We're ... kind of lost,' I sniffed. Lester nodded to himself, like a pat on the back to celebrate that he'd been right to stop and ask us. 'And we've lost our friend too. He was here and then he wasn't and we don't know where he is and he could be anywhere and he's definitely going to be scared and I don't want anything bad to happen to him and it's all m-my fa—' My mouth clipped the rest of the sentence, my bottom lip trembling and cheeks tingling. Lester's face looked grim. So did Michael's.

'What he's trying to say,' Bell said, taking over, 'is that we could do with some help. Directions or something.'

Lester looked deep in thought, his eyes narrowed and nose crinkled. Michael side-eyed him in the silence, wondering what he should do next. 'And your parents?' he said eventually, realizing Lester still hadn't reached his conclusion.

'Well ... you see, they ... well, they don't know we're

243

here,' Bell said quietly, clearly hoping we could skip over this part.

When Lester and Michael shared a horrified look, she quickly launched into an explanation about how we'd ended up in London and why, about Dad and me and how we were trying to find something to fix what had accidentally been broken. She didn't even try to gloss over anything or dress it up so it didn't look so bad. She just sighed and went full throttle, pedal to the metal and to hell if we got in trouble now. When she'd finished, she planted her hands on her hips and a somewhat stern look on her face, almost like it was Lester and Michael's fault that we'd lost Seb. Even I was a little scared to mess with Bell in that particular moment.

But Lester and Michael didn't grab us and cart us off to the nearest police station. In fact, they didn't even blink at most of it. Instead, Lester crouched down so we were at eye level – except he was quite short, so he ended up having to look up at us – and gave us both a little nudge on the shoulder.

'We're gonna find your friend, okay? And then we'll find your *other* friends and get you home safe and sound. But not before you've had the best Pride day you could

ask for. We can't send you home not wanting to come back!' Lester smiled warmly and, despite the incredibly terrible circumstances, I smiled too. We finally had some backup.

CHAPTER 25

NEW FRIENDS

Now, I have to say, under regular circumstances, it is not at all advisable to go wandering off with two strangers. In fact, you should never *ever* do that. It goes against all good common sense. But Lester and Michael seemed willing to help and at that moment, we didn't really have much choice.

So, the plan from that moment was simple – Lester and Michael would take us to the archway near Buckingham Palace (Michael, who's something of a history nerd, told us it was actually called the Admiralty Arch and is very, very old). Once we were there, we'd hopefully, fingers and toes crossed, find Seb, as well as Oscar and Dean. It was too simple really, which made me instantly suspicious. Things hadn't exactly gone in our favour so far. Who was to say that this plan wouldn't go wrong at the drop of a hat?

The crowd around us was more of a wave, surging towards Pride in a whirl of colour. Floating along in the middle of it all was quite dizzying. A giddy sensation took over me, like mini fireworks were being set off in my tummy. Being together with Michael and Lester (and their infectious excitement) didn't stop me from thinking about Seb, or worrying about everything going wrong, but it softly thawed the impending doom, like clothes on a radiator set out to dry.

On the walk, Bell finally had to ask. I could see it had been eating her up from the minute we'd set eyes on Lester and Michael, the question flashing a neon sign in the middle of her forehead.

'So, like, what's with the face?' She said it a little more abruptly than she meant and hastily added, 'It looks great, obviously.'

Lester let out a belly laugh so loud and booming that I was sure Mum might've heard it from back home.

'It's our make-up for the day,' he uttered between fits of laughter. Michael giggled along beside him. Lester pulled

himself together, spread his arms wide and said royally, 'We're drag queens, daaaaahling.'

I looked at Bell uncertainly and was happy to see I wasn't the only one who had no clue what that meant. Michael saw the glance we exchanged and laughed some more. Everything seemed to be funny to them and their happiness was infectious. It would've been more so if Seb wasn't missing.

'Drag queens,' Michael said, as if it were the most obvious thing in the world. 'We dress up in wigs and make-up and entertain the masses.'

'And *some* of us perform live for a living too,' Lester added smugly. 'We don't just stand around looking pretty, although that has been a known occupation.'

'You've caught us at an awkward time,' said Michael, patting the tape on his head. 'We haven't finished getting ready yet, but we're already running late for the parade so we didn't have much choice.'

Lester signalled to the large suitcase Michael was pulling behind him. 'The rest of the stuff is in there. I personally never feel complete without my wig and brows on, so I feel something like a naked mole rat right now.'

With shock, Bell and I both noticed that neither Lester

nor Michael had any eyebrows! It should've been obvious, but we'd completely missed it. Lester and Michael laughed so hard that they had to stop and hold onto each other. People passing by us joined in too, unable to resist the contagious laughter. One, an older man with greying hair and glasses that erupted in plastic rainbows on either side, even stopped to offer Michael and Lester a cough drop just in case. By the time they were done, the two of us were giggling too.

'We draw them on,' Lester said between shaky breaths, trying to get himself back under control. 'They look much better that way, believe me. You'll see them when we're done and you'll be amazed, mark my words. Michael draws the best brows in the business.' Michael looked proud at this.

'I'm not really much of a performer, though,' Michael said. 'Tonight will be my first ever show.' He looked like he might be sick at the thought, but Lester patted him on the back encouragingly.

'He'll bring the house down, you just watch.'

'What's the show?' I asked, happy for a distraction. The London Eye wasn't in sight any more but signs pointed out that Buckingham Palace wasn't far, which made my heart beat faster.

'Well, there's the parade first, of course. Michael and I

are walking with a bunch of our sisters.' Lester shimmied his shoulders, the sun catching his face and making it sparkle even more. 'Then we're on stage at the Southbank later this evening.'

'Sounds like fun!' Bell enthused while I nodded along in agreement.

'Fun? It's gay Christmas, of course it's going to be fun!' Lester gave us a wink, although Michael still looked like he might puke at the thought of his performance. He was only shaken out of it when a rainbow flag the size of a football pitch passed over our heads, the people under it reaching up with glee to push it down the street.

'What's the deal with you two anyway?' Lester asked, sizing us up properly for the first time. 'You said something about your dad?'

Bell pointed at me and I shrugged. 'Things have been weird lately,' I started carefully. It wasn't in my nature to talk to strangers or people I didn't know that well, but Lester and Michael made me feel safe.

'Ever since Dad said he was gay, things have just changed between us is all. I thought if I came here ... I might be able to fix it.' I said it warily, now unsure if it had ever been a good idea.

'Michael's mum is a lesbian,' Lester said, whipping a packet of chewing gum from his pocket and biting the wrapper until a piece fell into his mouth. He blew a bubble for good measure.

Michael nodded proudly. 'She came out last year. Nobody had a clue before then.'

My ears perked up at that. 'She did?'

Michael nodded some more. I was concerned how much his neck might ache when the day was done. 'Yep. She was married to my dad for donkey's years. After he died, she was alone for a little while and I didn't think she'd ever be happy again.' Michael's eyes darkened at the thought, the glimmer in them extinguished.

'She sat me down last winter and said she'd found somebody who makes her happy and that somebody just so happened to be another woman.' Michael and Lester shared a knowing smile, like some inside joke that went straight over mine and Bell's heads.

'And then what?' I asked thirstily, bouncing around people in the street and trying not to trip over Michael's suitcase.

'And then ...' Michael frowned, mulling it over for a moment. 'Then nothing. Nothing really changed after that. Sure, it was a little awkward at the beginning, mostly because it was something new. I think my mum wanted to make sure that I was okay more than anything. But time moved on and we all got used to it and now it's just … well, it's normal I suppose, whatever that means.'

Michael stopped, smack-bang in the middle of the street. Bell actually fell onto the suitcase, it was so abrupt. Michael rooted around in his pocket, his tongue between his teeth as he extracted his wallet. He flipped it open and spun it around so we could see. There, grinning back at us, were two women, their arms slung loosely around each other. It was sunny, but nothing was brighter than those two smiles.

'That's my mum,' Michael said, prouder than ever now. He didn't really need to point her out – she was the spitting image of him except, you know, a woman. She had short, greyish hair that lit up white where the sun caught it.

'And that's Dora, right there.' Michael pointed again, pushing the picture closer to our faces so we could get a proper look. Dora was tanned, with perfectly straight, pearly teeth that any dentist would be proud of. Her black hair was ruler-straight and touched her hips.

'She's pretty,' Bell said, and Michael lit up at that.

'I'm just glad she's happy now,' he said, flipping the wallet back into his pocket. 'She gets to live her life the way she wants to. She's happy, so I'm happy.' His grin was exactly the same as his mum's, with matching creases at either side.

'You said you're struggling to get things right again with your dad?' Lester said, still blowing bubbles around his words. I nodded, my short-lived joy popped like a balloon. 'Viv will be there today. You should talk to her,' said Lester, nodding at Michael who, of course, nodded with great enthusiasm right back.

'Yeah! Mum's lovely, she'd be happy to talk to you, I'm sure.'

The day ahead didn't seem so bad any more, like the rolling waves back home settling down after a storm. Seb was still lost, and Oscar and Dean were probably having kittens somewhere at the thought of us running wild in London without them. But the void between Dad and me suddenly didn't look so daunting. In fact, it almost seemed like a bridge was beginning to form that would bring us back to where we were. It gave me a fire, a determination to make everything right again. I was ready to fix all that had gone wrong today. I was ready to get things back on track.

CHAPTER 26

THE ARCHWAY IN THE MIDDLE OF LONDON

As is so often the case in London, or so I'm told, you round a corner and suddenly something's just *there*, plonked down in front of you as if conjured out of thin air. That was exactly what happened when Buckingham Palace appeared next to us. I hadn't noticed it at first, what with us walking around the side of it before getting to the front. I had thought it was just a rather big and splendid-looking house, maybe a manor, or one of those buildings that looks like a house on the outside but is actually just a bunch of offices on the inside and nothing all that exciting.

But as we trod the weaving pavement around the railings, alongside everybody else making their way towards Pride, a magnificent gate rose to greet us, the golden spikes at the top glinting in the sun. The palace, in all its royalty, bore down on us proudly, the sheer size enough to make us ogle in awe. It was an over-the-top and dramatic affair, with people pressed up against the black railings, gazing at the majesty of it all. Me and Bell couldn't help but get swept up in it, jumping up and down to try and get a better view of the palace. Bell swore blind that she caught a glimpse of the Queen looking down from one of the windows, but if you ask me it was probably just a shadow, or maybe one of those guards in the funny hats.

Lester kept checking the time, though, while Michael shuffled impatiently. They were too nice to hurry us on, but I caught them exchanging a look behind our backs when they thought I couldn't see. They were more than happy when we hopped back down onto the pavement, ready to get going once more.

The road from Buckingham Palace down towards Trafalgar Square and the Admiralty Arch is a long one, straighter than a ruler and wide as an ocean. According to Lester and Michael, they close it for special events, and today, with Pride and all of its celebrations taking centre stage in London, there were no cars in sight. People milled around in the middle of the road without a care in the world, snapping pictures of the palace behind us and the leafy park that sits next to it, which basically acts as the Queen's front lawn. It's a pretty impressive garden, although I wouldn't like strangers galloping around in front of my house if I were her.

It takes much longer to get down the road, which is actually called The Mall, than you'd think. But just when I was beginning to wonder if we were going in the right direction because surely we should be there by now, I heard a bass so strong that it moved the thick summer air around us. It was more of a *WHOMP!* that buzzed across your skin like electricity. I glanced at Bell, mild panic and definite excitement erupting between us.

Lester and Michael could feel it too. The closer we got, the more bounce appeared in their step and the bigger their smiles became. The sound had gotten clearer, morphing into music with the dull roar of a large crowd providing the backing vocals. There was a brief lull, where the people ahead parted to allow a bike to pass, and that's when I saw it – the Admiralty Arch, just ahead of us, as tall and marvellous as the palace we'd just left. People were snaking their way through it and out to the other side,

where Pride awaited.

'Come on!' Bell whooped, picking up her stride and beginning to run. 'He must be under there, I'm sure of it!'

I began running too, almost certain that Seb would be waiting with Oscar and Dean. We reached the arch together, scanning the faces of everyone around us. Lester and Michael looked at us expectantly, not knowing who they were looking for or what they looked like.

The people around us ambled underneath the arch and beyond, dressed in their colourful best and most with rainbows on or around them. It reminded me a little of Vale Gate High, where no two people really looked the same. But as I spun around in a slow circle, my smile began to fade. Seb wasn't here, and neither were Oscar and Dean. These people were all strangers. I couldn't see the green of Dean's hair or the casual lean of Oscar, and I definitely couldn't see the panicked face of my best friend. What if Seb was well and truly lost and we couldn't find him again? What would we do? My mind picked up the thread and ran, unravelling my thoughts so quickly that I found myself suddenly breathless.

'Maybe we're just early,' Bell said, although she didn't sound that convinced.

'They'll be around here somewhere, I'm sure,' Michael said gently. 'And we'll help you find them, right, Lez?' Lester looked like he wanted to say something but he thought better of it and nodded instead.

'Of course. We won't stop until we find them.' He looked out towards the crowd on the other side of the Admiralty Arch, hundreds and hundreds of people, probably thousands. 'We're going to need a plan, though,' Lester said, one already formulating in his eyes.

'What about the parade?' Bell murmured in a small voice. 'You're supposed to be in it.'

'That's not important,' Lester said, with a flick of his hand, and Michael nodded harder than ever. 'Pride is all about family, so if you're going to do this day properly, we're going to find your friends first.'

Michael dug out his phone. 'Shall I call backup?'

Lester nodded, his face set with fierce determination. 'Let's get this show on the road.'

Michael and Lester leaped straight into action, both scrolling and tapping their phones fervently, a determined intensity blazing in their eyes. 'Call Paulo and Liz, tell them to take our spot in the parade,' Lester murmured. Michael immediately prodded his screen and brought the phone up to his ear. When the person on the other end picked up, he turned his back and began talking fast.

'Do you have a picture of your friends?' Lester asked, still not looking up from his own phone. It took us a minute to realize he was even talking to us. Bell found a picture of Seb on her phone, one where he didn't look on the verge of a panic attack. When I leaned over to see which picture she'd chosen, I felt a tiny *whoosh* in the pit of my stomach. Seb's glasses were on the tip of his nose and he was beaming at the camera, me and Bell on either side of him and Mack's Arcade behind us, its flashing lights frozen in time. Lester took a snap of the picture and did some more tapping.

'What about the other friends? Do you have a picture of them?' he murmured distractedly.

I shook my head at the exact same time as Bell. 'It can't be hard to spot them, though,' I said quickly. 'Dean's got green hair, you can't really miss . . .' The words trailed away from me as I noticed the people all around us – there was hair in every shade, including lots of green. I was starting to think you'd be more out of place in London if you had a natural hair colour.

'Done,' Lester said, as Michael bounced back over. 'I've got every queen I can think of on high alert to keep an eye

out for your friends. If a drag queen in a three-mile radius sees them, they'll let us know.'

We all breathed. Even though we were in the middle of London with Pride happening no more than a couple of metres away, it felt like I was listening to it happen underwater. Fear had taken Seb's spot between me and Bell – and, unfortunately, it didn't look like that was going to get lost anytime soon.

I remembered then that, somewhere in the city, Dad was here too. I wondered what he was doing, if we were actually somewhere close together but had no idea that the other was only around the corner. Another wave of sadness threatened to rise in my throat but I pushed it back down. Now wasn't the time.

'So ... now what?' Bell said, flicking her eyes over me and then over to Lester.

'We shouldn't get too far from here, you know, in case one of your friends shows up looking for you guys.' Lester looked over to the crowd, mushed together with their backs to us. Beyond was a lot of noise, although I couldn't quite see where it was coming from.

'There's no harm in watching some of the parade while we wait for backup, right?' Michael peered over at the crowds too, his eyes brightening a little. 'It might cheer you up a little while we wait.'

I hesitated, looking around us once more in hope that Seb was about to appear. But, of course, he was nowhere in sight. So, armed with the knowledge that backup was on its way, whatever that meant, we left the Admiralty Arch to inspect the parade. Despite everything, the thrill and excitement in the air was infectious. Bell clutched onto my arm, peering at the wonders around us. There were people everywhere, some dressed in colours so bright that the sun would've had every right to be jealous. There were young people and old people, ones who'd barely learned how to walk and those who needed something or someone to hold onto to get more than three paces. Faces painted with make-up rivalled even that of Lester and Michael, whose own faces had somehow stayed pristine and glowing. At one point, they both paused to mist their faces with some spray from a can.

'Much better,' Lester said, admiring his own reflection in a pocket-sized mirror as Michael did the same.

We fought our way through the crowds, which were deeper than I'd first thought, the music getting closer and closer. Lester went first, sneakily moving people far enough out of our way that there was a clear path for us all, but not enough that those people noticed or cared. Bell went next, holding onto Lester's T-shirt. I followed, refusing to let go of Bell's shoulder – I'd already lost three people today, I didn't need to lose a fourth – and Michael took up the back, making sure that we all stayed together.

My panic started to set in when we reached the front, where a metal barrier kept us away from the road. If I looked to my right, there were thousands of people. If I looked to my left, there were thousands more. And, if I looked across the road to the other side, there were more people than I could possibly comprehend. Lester and Michael didn't seem too fussed about the fanfare and were instead already swaying and bouncing to the beat of the music.

Bell searched the faces in the crowd around us and I did too, hoping Seb would just magically appear. But our search didn't get very far because that's when the parade sprang to life.

CHAPTER 27

THE PARADE

I don't know where to start with the parade. I would usually say starting at the beginning is always wise, but considering we'd already missed a fair chunk of it, that would be impossible. I'll do my best to explain what we saw but forgive me if I don't do the best job. My eyes could only see so much at once, and even then, they almost didn't believe what was right in front of them.

According to the rainbow squiggle on the flyer's map, which I'd obsessed over so much that it was now imprinted on the back of my eyelids, we were near the end of the parade route, right next to Trafalgar Square. When we had reached the front of the crowd, everything had kind of been on pause, a lull in the parade as others caught up.

A marching band in multicoloured uniforms were standing still, as if their lives depended on being frozen to the spot. Their instruments, gleaming gold and magnificent in the sun, looked so heavy that I wondered how on Earth they could be carried from the beginning of the map's route all the way to the end. I didn't fancy my chances carrying one of those instruments further than the end of the street and back, and even that might be a stretch.

Before I could gawk any more at the scene before us, a harsh whistle blew and everything came to life, wonderfully chaotic things happening in every direction. The band raised their instruments like they were weapons that meant business. On the sound of the next whistle, they all took a deep breath and began playing. The sound was enormous, notes of elation spiralling up above us and spilling over the crowd like an overflowing bathtub. It was met with a cheer so loud, I was sure that the Earth moved beneath my feet. Bell gripped my hand tightly, mirroring my amazement at what we were seeing. Then the band began to march forward and the parade lingering behind them started to proceed.

Behind the band was a large white truck. It had maybe seen better days, but it had been draped and decorated with spray paint and flags so it wouldn't have looked out of place in one of our *Mario Kart* battles. A small collection of people, with faces that looked like they'd been painted with the rainbow itself, stood on a trailer connected to the back from which impossibly loud music was pumping. They held onto the rails of the truck as it began to creep forward, waving to the crowd and jumping up and down with more joy than I knew was possible. One woman, in particular, seemed to be having such a good time that she was doing the Macarena to a beat that apparently only she could hear.

A crowd of people were dancing behind the truck, holding up balloons in various colours. The balloons were contorted into shapes that looked suspiciously like a famous mouse with famous ears. They were dancing to the music, dressed in the same T-shirts imprinted with a rainbow version of the mouse that the balloons were imitating. One person skipped out to the side of the crowd and did a cartwheel and we all whooped and hooted over that.

Behind the mouse people, there were feathers. Tons

and tons of feathers, clinging to people from head to toe and forming wondrously dramatic outfits. One man in particular, who didn't appear to be wearing many clothes besides the feathers, walked in a grand zigzag, slowly sashaying in the midst of his pod like a regal snake. His feathers stretched far above his head, reaching for the skies above. I couldn't help but think that we would never have lost Seb if we'd put him in one of those.

A fire engine came rolling along after the feathers, blaring its horn from time to time and flashing its lights over the crowd. But, instead of being red as expected, this truck had been painted in swirls of colour.

LONDON PRIDE

had been splashed across it in large bubble-font writing. Firefighters leaned out of the windows, waving and whistling, and those who weren't in the truck were walking along beside it. One of the walkers gave Lester a wink, much to his joy. Bell nearly barfed at that and then we both fell into a fit of giggles.

'I just love it,' Michael said as we pushed our way back through the crowd towards the arch once more. A man in rainbow underpants sprinted past, yelling 'HAPPY PRIDE' at the top of his lungs. Bell first looked thoroughly disgusted but burst out laughing as he leaped past the crowd and did the splits in mid-air. Michael clutched his chest lovingly. 'Pride really is my favourite time of year.'

'Did someone mention gay Christmas?' said a soft voice behind us. Michael spun around and leaped into someone's arms, whooping and hollering.

'All right, Viv?' Lester grinned, also coming in for a hug. 'What do you think of the mug?' I frowned and waited for Lester to produce a kitchen cup. Fortunately for me, nobody else noticed my confusion because I later found out that mug apparently meant face. Don't worry, I still don't get it either.

'Stunning,' Viv said with pride, peeling herself away

from Michael and admiring them both. 'And who've we got here?' she asked, peeking over Michael's shoulder and seeing me and Bell standing awkwardly behind him.

'Oh! Mum, this is Archie and Bell. It's their first Pride!' Michael's mum beamed at that, but her smile disappeared quickly when Michael continued. 'They're having some trouble. They've lost their friends and we can't find them anywhere.'

Michael and Lester quickly explained the story. When Lester mentioned my dad, I squirmed a little under Viv's watchful and concerned eye. 'Are you both okay?' she asked when they'd finished.

Bell nodded immediately, as I'd known she would. She's not one to say when something's wrong, even if it clearly is. I just kind of shrugged and grimaced at the same time. Viv watched me carefully, an odd look etched on her face in the form of gentle frown lines.

'Well, first of all we have to find their friends,' she said.

'Genius! Why didn't we think of that?!' Lester grinned as Viv rolled her eyes, which were covered in glitter.

'I think if we tell the police th—'

'NO!' I yelped, louder than I'd meant to. I held my hands up in apology. 'Sorry, I just … I don't want to

get anyone in trouble. It was my idea to come. I don't care if I get the blame, just please don't get the others in trouble too.'

'That's very noble of you, sweetheart, but your friend is lost in a big and strange city, and we have almost no chance of finding him by just wandering around and hoping to strike lucky.' To prove her point, a large party of people danced right past us, skipping and hooting at nothing in particular and clearly having a rather merry time. Viv ran a hand through her greyish-white hair and sighed, thinking quickly.

'If we just wait by the arch, he'll come. They'll all come, I'm sure of it!' I gestured wildly around us at Pride, like that would solve the problem and my friends would just spill out of the crowd with smiles on their faces. But the desperation did little to convince anybody. Viv studied me sympathetically.

'Do you mind if you all give us a moment,' she finally said, nodding at me. 'We'll just be a minute. Why don't you lot go over to the arch and see if any of those friends have arrived yet.' Viv gently guided me away from the crowds behind us, who were still yelling with delight at the passing parade.

'I just wanted to ask if you're all right, darling,' she said gently. 'You know, *really* all right. It sounds like you and your family have been through a lot recently.'

We stopped a little way from the crowd, the arch still in sight. I could see Bell and Lester giggling together but no sign of Seb, or Oscar and Dean. Viv waited patiently, her thoughtful eyes creased at the edges by a warm smile.

'I'm okay,' I said automatically, even if it wasn't strictly true. I was starting to realize that it hadn't been true for a while now.

'That's what Michael used to say,' Viv laughed. *'I'm okay, Mum, I promise!'* Her imitation was spot on, which made me smile and relax a little. 'He would've sworn blind that there was nothing wrong because he didn't want to upset me, but I know my son better than anybody and I know when something's up.' Viv tapped her nose and winked.

'What I'm trying to say, Archie, is that it's okay to not be okay. What Michael and Lester said about your dad, it'd be understandable if you were confused or upset or had a million and one questions that you don't know how to put into words. That's normal!' Viv paused, choosing her words carefully. 'I don't want to speak out of turn or say anything that I have no right in saying, so you just tell me to mind my own business if I do. But, if I may, I'd like to say something.'

She paused. I thought it was for dramatic effect but I realized she was waiting for me to give her the green light, so I nodded quickly. Viv glanced over at Michael before continuing, a small smile pulling at the corners of her mouth.

'When I told Michael about Dora, it was the hardest thing I think I've ever had to do. I went over and over it for days, which turned into weeks, and before I knew it, it had been six months and I still didn't know what I wanted to say or how I wanted to say it. I didn't want to upset Michael, especially after everything that had happened with his dad, and I didn't want things between us to change. All I knew was that life was passing me by and that living with such a secret is no way to be happy. And that's all I wanted – to be happy, like everybody else.'

Viv puffed out a vague laugh at the memory. 'I sat down and thought about what's most important to me – the answer was Michael *and* Dora. When I looked at everything else, it just paled in comparison. I could lose everything tomorrow, and so long as I had Michael and Dora by my side, I'd be the happiest person under the sun.

'When I told Michael, I started and I stuttered my way through it like I didn't know how to speak words. And sure, when it was all done, things were a little awkward for a minute. But I never loved him any less, and I don't think he loved me any less either. It was just something new, and change takes some getting used to.'

Viv paused, collecting her thoughts together. 'One thing I've learned since then is that life can be delicate and frail, but it can also be full of colour and wonder. You just have to let it in. And you must! You must let it in! I don't know anything about your dad, but I do know that he's probably just as confused and scared about everything as you've been. And I'd bet my last penny that he still loves you just as much. In fact, this whole thing might've made him realize that he loves you even more.'

I felt my insides pinch together at that. I thought about the picture of me and Dad stuffed in my bag, about everything that had happened over the last couple of weeks to get us here, to this moment, at Pride searching for answers. And maybe I'd just found them.

'I'm rambling now, forgive me,' Viv laughed. 'But while I'm at it, I'll just finish with this. I have never been happier than I am right now. It took me fifty years and some change to feel this way, to feel this complete. But, when I really think about it, I'm no different than I was. Being in love with Dora hasn't changed me one bit. Now, I almost feel a silly for thinking that the world would implode over something so small. When your dad told you he was gay, did the world stop spinning? Did the stars fall out of the sky?'

I shook my head and Viv beamed back at me. 'Exactly! Nothing changed at all! It might take some getting used to, and sure, it might be a little awkward at first. But I promise you one thing – your dad is still your dad and that's never going to change.'

I tried to make sense of everything Viv had just said, turning the words the right way up after they'd tumbled through my ears. Even as I tried to grasp them properly, I knew one thing – Viv's speech certainly beat the bakery and cakes that Oscar had been talking about. She gave me a gentle pat on the shoulder, grinning from ear to ear.

'Now, we just have to find your fr—'

'WAIT RIGHT THERE!' a loud voice yelled in manic desperation over the dull roar of the crowd. 'DON'T YOU MOVE A MUSCLE, ARCHIBALD ALBRIGHT!'

I spun around and nearly fainted with happiness. His

face might have been red-hot with rage, but you couldn't mistake the tinge of relief in his voice. Oscar and Dean had finally found us.

CHAPTER 28

BACK ON TRACK – WELL, KINDA

Despite the fact that there were dozens of people between us, all of whom could've formed potential trip hazards, Oscar refused to look anywhere else but directly at me. He stormed towards us, sweating enough to fill a bucket or two. Loose strands of his hair, usually scruffy and fluffy and with a life of its own, were plastered to his forehead like he had been caught in a dreadful downpour.

'Ohhh, he doesn't look like a happy bunny,' Viv murmured, as Oscar nearly lost a fight with a parked pushchair. 'Please tell me this is one of the friends we're missing?'

'Yep, that's Oscar,' I said, a little nervous now that I could see the frenzy on his face. A sudden thought flashed across my mind – he didn't know about Seb yet. That was going to be a fun story to try and explain.

'WHERE – IN GOD'S NAME – HAVE YOU BEEN?!' Oscar puffed and spluttered, grabbing me by the shoulders and giving me a frantic shake.

'More importantly, where have *you* been?' Bell said, sidling up next to me with Michael and Lester in tow.

'LOOKING – FOR YOU – EVERYWHERE!!!!' Oscar looked all of five seconds away from keeling over and hitting the pavement with an unhealthy thud, so I tried to put a smile on my face to let him know that everything was okay. He took a deep breath and his shoulders sagged a little.

'We couldn't find you at the station,' Dean said, catching up to us and slightly out of breath. Despite his dishevelled hair – now resembling tufts of green grass which had been pulled this way and that – he was still a little more together than Oscar, who was practically vibrating on the spot. 'We looked everywhere but you were nowhere to be seen.'

'*We* were looking for *you*,' Bell said, more accusingly than I'm sure she'd meant it. She stood with her hands on her hips while Michael and Lester looked sheepishly at the floor like they were interrupting something private.

Oscar took another deep breath, his eyes half-shut and his hands stretched out into thin air. He counted to ten, slow and steady, and when he opened his eyes again, he looked a little more like himself. Flustered, sure, but definitely more calm.

'How about we sit down and you can tell me *exactly* what happened. I've been losing my mind since we got here.' Oscar, without waiting for a response, kicked some rubbish out of his way and flopped down in exhaustion. Once we were all sat down, we took it in turns to recount what had happened.

As it turned out, Dean and Oscar had gotten separated themselves in the mad rush at the station. Both had thought that the other would be with the three of us, but when they eventually found each other outside, we were nowhere to be seen. They'd panicked, of course, and run frantically from one decision to another in their plan to try and find us. When they'd exhausted every possible solution at the train station and were deliberating calling the police – and our parents, much to my and Bell's horror – they remembered the Admiralty Arch.

'We weren't even going to come here because we were adamant you guys wouldn't remember the meeting spot, much less be able to make it here on your own,' Dean said offhandedly while Bell glowered next to me. I felt the force with which she was trying to hold in a defiant rebuttal. It was vibrating off her in waves.

'But what happened to you guys?' Oscar asked, before Bell could fire back a response. 'What on Earth have you been doing?'

Bell took the noble duty of recounting our story, although she conveniently left out the part where we lost Seb and had so far failed to find him. I was only mildly concerned that Oscar and Dean hadn't appeared to realize that there were only two of us here instead of the three they'd lost, but I didn't fancy shaking that beehive just yet.

'And that's when we met Lester and Michael, who helped us get to the arch,' Bell finished with a nonchalant shrug. Lester and Michael smiled awkwardly, knowing full well that we were keeping a secret.

'And where's the little one?' Dean said, leaning around Bell as if Seb might be hiding behind her.

'You're up, Archie,' Bell said, patting me on the back. Well, I guess it had been my fault that we'd ended up in this mess, so it was my responsibility to rip the plaster off.

Oscar had finally seemed so relieved, it almost felt like a shame to have to rock the boat again.

'About that,' I said, as cheerfully as I could. Oscar froze, as if he had peeked behind the curtain and read the words I was rehearsing in my head.

'Don't you dare say it,' Oscar breathed, the panic returning in full force now. He looked over our heads, his eyes feverishly scanning the nearby crowds. 'Please tell me he's gone to get ice cream and will be back here any minute,' he said out of the corner of his mouth, his teeth clamped together.

'Not quite.' I shuffled nervously. 'You see, when we lost you guys, we got a little sidetracked on our way to the arch and . . . well, we kind of . . . you know . . .' I trailed off under Oscar's fearful glare. Dean dropped his head into his hands and gave an empty laugh, although I couldn't quite see what was so funny myself.

'We lost Seb,' Bell interjected, just to make sure we were all on the same page. 'But, who knows, maybe he *is* getting ice cream from somewhere.'

She tried to smile but it withered as Oscar, rather dramatically, slumped backwards and fainted on the spot.

CHAPTER 29

BUTTERCUP, QUEEN
OF THE QUEENS

We all sat in a semicircle of silence as Viv, who had put her mum-hat on, handed out bottles of water. She uncapped another, smaller bottle, and handed it to Oscar. 'For the shock, sweetheart,' she said with a wink and a grin. Oscar smiled back weakly, taking a short swig. He grimaced but shook it off.

It didn't take long for Dean to ask the common question of the day, one that I was sure I'd heard a million times since I'd got out of bed this morning a lifetime ago. 'So, now what?'

Everybody looked at each other, waiting for somebody else to take a leap and solve the problem. Considering I had already caused enough damage for one day, I thought it best that I keep my own mouth shut and wait for somebody with a little more authority – and sense – to offer up a solution.

Surprisingly, it was Michael who stood up and, even more shockingly, he was smiling. Lester leaned around to see what had caught his attention and leaped to his feet too, beaming with every tooth in his head.

'I hear we've got some trouble,' an impossibly tall stranger said. Crowds parted as he walked towards us, people gazing up at him in wonder and whispering behind their hands in awe. It was like a celebrity had landed in our midst. The stranger ignored the rumblings of the crowd and wrapped Michael and Lester up in a firm bear hug. His voice was deep and gruff, at odds with his face, which had been softly painted with every shimmer of the rainbow. His hair flowed in loose waves down to the middle of his back, a deep and dark red.

'It's a wig,' Viv whispered, as she saw me staring. 'But don't tell him I told you that.' She spread her arms wide and embraced him. 'Nice to see you again, darling.'

'Rumour has it you've only gone and *lost* a child,' the stranger said, feigning shock and horror with an over-the-top gasp. There was a lilt to his voice, like he found

something funny that the rest of us hadn't figured out yet. 'On the day of Pride too! Whatever will those straight people think of us!' His laugh was deep and booming and even louder than Lester's. It sounded like it was being played through one of the parade speakers.

'Guys, this is Buttercup,' Michael announced with pride.

Buttercup saw us mulling this over and laughed once more. 'You can call me Norman if you want to, that's on the birth certificate.'

'Buttercup's fine with me.' Bell shrugged.

'Ahhh, who's this angel! I like her already!' Bell blushed, which was a first.

'Buttercup is hosting the event we're performing at later,' Lester said, giving him a pat on the back. He put one hand around his mouth and, in a stage whisper, added, 'Some call him the queen of all drag queens, but that's just because he's the loudest.'

'In that case, that would make you my second-in-command,' Buttercup boomed, laughing some more. The projection to his voice was really quite impressive. 'Talking of which, we have a show to do this evening, so the quicker we solve this mystery, the better.' Buttercup looked at his watch and then at us expectantly.

'How do we even begin looking for one kid in this city, on the day of London Pride no less?' Dean said, looking almost as stressed as Oscar. 'It's like looking for a drop of water in the desert.'

Buttercup tutted and rolled his eyes, which looked heavy under all that paint. I was almost certain eyelashes couldn't be that long, but it seemed rude and unimportant to ask about them now.

'Never underestimate the powers of a drag queen, sir. And did you really think I was coming here alone?' Buttercup curled his lips and whistled loudly. Almost immediately and as if from nowhere, several people appeared.

Viv chuckled to herself. 'Looks like we've got some new recruits,' she said. 'And don't they look fabulous!'

Me, Bell, Dean and Oscar watched in slack-jawed disbelief as Buttercup stood up even taller than before and performed an official roll call, gesturing to each new friend in turn.

There was Yan, who had buzzed his eyebrows off so his face kind of shone in the sunlight. He didn't smile much, or even say much for that matter. Instead, he quietly assessed the situation, nodding to himself at regular intervals. 'Nice to meet you,' he said in a delicate tone when Buttercup introduced him.

Then there were Lita and Lara, twin sisters with wispy, lavender-coloured hair. This was the only way to tell them apart by looking at them – Lita's hair was bunched up into two messy knots on either side of her head, a little like headphones but made of hair, whereas Lara's had been buzzed incredibly short at the sides with only a flop of purple on top. They linked arms next to Buttercup, gazing at him adoringly and chattering between themselves in melodic whispers.

At barely a notch older than Oscar and Dean, Boo was the youngest of the lot, and also the shortest. They barely came up to Michael's shoulder, even when they were bouncing up and down with excitement next to him. Buttercup announced that it was their first Pride, just like it was mine and Bell's. Boo, flushed with enthusiasm, talked at a million miles an hour, like the world might end before they'd had a chance to finish their sentence. 'Incredible to meet you all,' they beamed. 'Isn't this going to be fun!'

Finally, there was Dora, who I recognized from the picture Michael had shown us earlier. She gave Michael and Lester a quick hug and hello before slipping her hand into Viv's and planting a gentle kiss on her cheek. Viv smiled warmly and squeezed her hand a little tighter.

So, there we were, a huddle of thirteen people: me and Bell, Oscar and Dean, Lester and Michael, Viv and Dora, Lita and Lara, Yan and Boo, and, of course, Buttercup. I took us all in, a group of colourful warriors ready to go to war donning make-up and wigs, glitter and sparkle as our weapons and armour. I felt stronger and safer than I had all day.

Being the queen of all drag queens – or so Lester told us – it was Buttercup who we all looked to for instructions, but even he seemed to be struggling with what to do next.

'How about we just split up?' Oscar said desperately.

'And look for clues? Doesn't *that* always pan out well?' Bell murmured in my ear. I stifled a giggle.

But Buttercup nodded and got out his phone. 'We all need a picture of what this kid looks like, so let's start there. And what's his name, please? I doubt we'll get far calling him "this kid".'

'Seb,' said Bell, offering up the picture she'd shown Michael and Lester earlier.

Buttercup divided us into smaller groups – he had to

remind Boo that these were not 'teams' as we were not playing a game and that this was serious. Boo stopped bouncing for a second and mumbled an apology, but they began skipping around the circle again less than a heartbeat later.

By the time we were ready to begin our search and rescue mission, there were five groups ready and raring to go. Oscar and Dean refused to take their eyes off of us, so me and Bell were going with them. Viv and Dora were set to go in one direction, while Lester and Michael were ready to go in another. Lara and Lita clasped hands with Yan and prepared to venture out into the crowds. Much to Boo's excitement, they were going with Buttercup.

'We meet back here in an hour, okay?' Buttercup said. 'And if we don't find Seb in that time, then we have to go to the police. That's the deal, all right?'

Me and Bell shared a terrified look, mirrored by Oscar and Dean, but we all knew that there wasn't any other choice. Seb had already been lost for over two hours now, and the longer the day went on, the smaller our chances were of finding him. If I had to get grounded for the rest of my life just to find my best friend again, I was more than willing to make that sacrifice.

'See you back here soon then,' Buttercup said. Without

another word, he reached into the folds of his dress and produced a megaphone. He saw me and Bell gaping and chuckled to himself. 'Like a Mary Poppins handbag under all this glamour.'

Buttercup took one big breath and flicked a switch.

'WE ARE LOOKING FOR A **LOST CHILD!**

HAVE YOU SEEN A LOST CHILD?

HIS NAME IS SIMON!'

Boo pulled on Buttercup's sleeve.

'SORRY, HIS NAME IS SEB! HAVE YOU SEEN A LOST CHILD CALLED SEB?! EXCUSE ME, MA'AM, NO PICTURES RIGHT NOW, THIS IS AN EMERGENCY! OH, YOU DO? IT'S CUSTOM-MADE BUT YOU CAN FIND SOMETHING SIMILAR IN PRIMARK, I'M SURE!'

Buttercup strode off into the crowd with purpose, wielding the megaphone like a sword and parting onlookers once more, Boo galloping along beside him. Lita and Lara swept brushes across their cheeks, which suddenly gleamed even brighter than before, reflecting back at us all blindingly. They added a slick of the magic to Yan's face with delight before slinking off together.

'I guess this is it,' Bell said, watching the others go.

Our search-and-rescue mission was about to step up a gear.

CHAPTER 30

AN UNEXPECTED RECRUIT

It was hard to stay optimistic that we would accomplish our mission and find Seb when our search party included Oscar. His eyes were wild with panic, and he would jump in the air every three seconds like he had just been electrocuted.

'I thought I saw him,' he'd say with each eruption, disappointment mixed with yet more panic clouding his face once again.

On the fiftieth occasion, or maybe it was the hundredth, Bell spun around in a huff. 'Will you please CALM DOWN! You're not helping!'

Oscar, clearly stung, muttered something that only he could hear. After that, we kept ploughing on in silence,

Pride happening in all of its joy around us. We'd decided not to search too far from the arch. Buttercup thought it was impossible that Seb could be a million miles away, especially considering the direction we'd been coming from in the first place. Viv and Dora had taken the task of heading back to the train station just in case, while the rest of us spread out around the arch and Trafalgar Square, hoping with all our might that one of us might just stumble across him.

The only problem was . . . we were in the busiest part of the parade. Trafalgar Square was filled with more people than I thought was possible, maybe even more than the population of my entire town. A large stage had been erected at one end, decorated with a bunch of flags that flew proudly over our heads. Someone who I had never heard of, but who Dean was particularly excited to see, was performing on the stage as we circled Trafalgar Square's edge. We could see her flipping her hair and belting into the microphone on one of the big screens.

'He definitely won't be in that chaos,' Bell said, standing up on her tiptoes on a low wall to get a better look. 'He would rather swim back home than go anywhere near a crowd this big.'

'Wait, maybe that's it!' Oscar said, bubbling with panic or excitement (I couldn't quite decide which one). 'He won't be anywhere near a crowd this big, right? So, we're already looking in the wrong place. We need somewhere close by that's quiet and open and . . .' Oscar trailed off.

'That could be anywhere in a mile radius,' Dean sighed, unconvinced by Oscar's apparent breakthrough. He ran a hand through his hair and sighed some more. 'We should've never let you come with us!' Dean suddenly erupted, all but spitting feathers. 'Why did we let you guys talk us into this?! If you three had just let us take you back, then we wouldn't be in this position! We'd all be at home having a grand old time with NOBODY lost in the middle of London without a hope in hell of finding them!'

I felt my face heat up and my bottom lip begin to tremble. Before I could say anything, though, Bell stepped in, because of course she wasn't about to take this lying down.

'Don't blame this on us! You're the adults here. All you had to say was no and we could've all turned around and gone straight back home. It's not our fault that *you* lost the three of us before we'd even got out of the train station!'

'How was it our fault?!' Dean snapped back. It was surprising that steam wasn't coming out of his ears at this point, but Bell wasn't backing down.

'Guys, please, stop it,' I said, but the argument continued over my head. Oscar tried to step in but Dean brushed him off. The fire in Bell's eyes, similar to the look she gets when she's reached the final level of a video game and is going in for the kill, said she wasn't about to quit either. So, I did the one thing that I knew would stop it – I burst into tears once more. Well, it was more noise than anything at first, but real tears soon came, along with a crushing hopelessness that washed over me in waves. Once the tears came, it was nearly impossible to stop.

'This is all my fault,' I said in between stuttering sobs, trying to hide my face in my hands. 'It was my stupid idea to come here, to try to fix things. But I haven't fixed things at all. I've only made it worse.' I tried to say something else, anything else to make this better, but the blubbing was in full force, building a wall at the back of my throat so the words couldn't find their way out.

'Archie?'

My head in my hands, and still sobbing somewhat hysterically, I heard the argument, and everyone involved, halt. For a second, all I could hear was the buzz of Pride around us, the incessant wailing of someone struggling to find their key on stage.

Then, again, 'Archie?'

The voice definitely didn't belong to Bell, and it couldn't belong to Oscar or Dean. For a wild moment, I almost let myself believe that the voice could be Seb's, but then I heard it again and realized with absolute certainty that it didn't belong to him either.

'Archie. Is that you?'

My heart seemed to recognize the voice before my head did, freezing in panic. The blood it pumped through my body ran icy cold. When I looked up from the safety of my hand-nest, it took a minute for my eyes to adjust to the bright sunlight. Things were a little blurry through the tears, but I saw Bell, absolute horror painted on her face. Oscar and Dean held each other upright, suddenly looking faint. As the picture became clearer, I saw that almost everybody was looking at something, or someone, in alarm.

'Archie? What on Earth are you doing here?'

I slowly turned around. Finally, my head pieced the picture together and I realized why my entire body felt numb.

'Hi, Dad,' I said, bottom lip still trembling, although now more out of fear. 'Fancy seeing you here.'

CHAPTER 31

BIG TROUBLE. HUGE, IN FACT

I looked at Dad. Dad looked at me. Everybody else looked at the awkward space between us, unsure what to do next, because surely if you just stand still and don't say anything, the bad dream will end and you'll wake up in bed like nothing has happened. I blinked quickly, but Dad didn't move or fade away, the scene didn't turn to black. I was very much awake and this was very much happening.

Dad's face was blank and unmoving, which somehow made everything worse. I couldn't see anger or confusion, or one single flicker that might give away what he was thinking. He just looked at me, unblinking, like he too thought I might be a bad dream or a glitch in the matrix.

We could've stood there for ten seconds or ten hours.

Time didn't seem to understand the concept of sticking to its usual routine and was instead watching us eagerly, forgetting to tick on at its usual pace. And was it just my ears, or the incessant *whoosh* of blood rushing to my head, that had silenced the noise around us? Was Pride still happening, or had it stopped to watch too?

'Archie?' Dad said again, almost in wonder and disbelief at what his eyes were showing him. Then he spotted Bell, uttering her name like it was a new language he was trying for the first time.

'Eliza Barclay Card the Fourth, I'm afraid you must be mistaken,' Bell said snootily, adopting her train station voice once more.

'He can see you standing right there,' Dean hissed.

'He wouldn't have done if you hadn't just told him,' Bell growled back.

Dad blinked, this time thought and feeling beginning to form. It crept across his face like the shadow cast from a setting sun, his eyebrows sliding into a frown. I could see realization building, one brick at a time, and acted quickly.

Now look, I'm not trying to give you pointers on how to get out of trouble. BUT, if you just so happened to be in trouble and you also just so happened to be trying to get out of it, knowing your parents' weak spot is always a good place to start. There are, of course, the basic rules to follow when you've been caught out on a lie, and they look a little something like this:

ARCHIE'S RULE BOOK FOR RULE BREAKING

1. Cry — it gives you time to think of a reasonable excuse as to why you broke the rules in the first place. Not to be confused with guilt-tripping. This is completely different, I swear.

2. Stand still and wait for a hole in the ground to swallow you up. If you pray hard enough, this should work.

3. Offer to do the dishes for a whole month. It's a heinous task that everybody hates, parents included. They'll forgive you if you offer to do it. Maybe ...

4. Pack your bags and move to Mars. It might

be the only option you have left, depending on what rule you broke.

5. Come clean immediately and hope for the best. Honesty is always the best policy, after all. Well, apparently.

For me, at that moment, the emphasis was on rule number one. I know my dad can't stand tears or overwhelming emotion. His resolve just crumbles. Yes, it was cruel of me to use that against him but ... look, it was that or be grounded for the rest of my life, and we had some rather pressing things to be getting on with at that particular moment.

So, I rushed across the space between us and threw myself at Dad with force, wrapping my arms around his middle and burying my face into the folds of his clothes. I didn't need to make myself cry – I already was. Instinctively, he pulled me in closer, rubbing comforting circles into my back.

'Hey, hey, hey, what's all this? What's happened? Are you okay?' Dad crouched down and hugged me properly.

'It's all my fault, Dad. I'm sorry,' I stuttered and sobbed

into the crook of his neck.

'What's your fault? What's happened? And what are you doing here?' Dad pulled away and assessed me properly. He looked more concerned than angry, but to be fair, he didn't know about Seb yet.

'I can explain, Kevin,' Oscar said, standing forward gallantly. Dad looked up at him, as if he'd only just realized that he and Dean were standing there. Then Dad noticed Bell again and his befuddlement grew.

'What the . . .' he managed, taking us all in.

'Maybe we should find somewhere a little quieter?' Dean suggested, a bounce in his voice. Oscar and Bell nodded in unison. I blew a snot bubble to show that I also thought it was a great idea. If we were going to get in trouble, being shouted at in front of thousands of spectators didn't exactly sound appealing.

Oscar leaned over and checked Dean's watch. 'I know just the place,' he said, and began walking back towards the Admiralty Arch, his fingers crossed firmly behind his back.

It wasn't until we were at the arch that I understood Oscar's sudden desperation to get back there. Sure, we were most definitely in trouble for our little jaunt into London without a responsible adult – it was clear from the day's events that neither Oscar nor Dean fitted into that category – but we'd almost certainly be in even bigger trouble if Dad realized we had lost Seb. I could only imagine the consequences of telling that story to Dad, how Dad would have to tell Seb's mum – a terrifying thought, much scarier than any movie Oscar could show us – and the whole thing sounded more horrific than I could bear.

But, back at the arch, there was still no sign of Seb, or any of the others for that matter. The hour was almost up. We were about to run out of time. My heart dropped down into my shoes and made friends with my toes, hiding in shame and beating in fear. What had happened to Seb? Where was he now?

Oscar checked the crowds around us nervously but there wasn't a drag queen in sight, just hordes of other people who had the nerve to still be having fun while my best friend was lost in this huge city.

'Does someone want to tell me what the hell's going on?' Dad said, his face setting into a stern expression now that he'd reassured himself that nobody was injured. Realization that we were here was clearly starting to set in

and he didn't look happy about it. He didn't look happy about it at all. He raised an eyebrow expectantly, now zeroing his attention in on me.

'Well . . .' I said, letting the word hang in the air while I waited for divine inspiration to strike. No lightning bolt came, so I tried saying it again, hoping that a sudden seed would turn into a thought that would help us get out of this mess. But, sometimes, even if you might get into trouble, it's best to just tell the truth. My parents used to say: 'What's the worst that can happen?' I was just hoping that Dad would remember that.

I started at the beginning. Well, kind of. I started at *our* beginning, I should say. I stuttered and stammered but my voice grew stronger as I went. I made sure to shoulder the blame at every hurdle, which wasn't exactly noble or brave – it was just the unfortunate truth.

Like Bell had done earlier, I left out the bit about Seb. I also took a short cut around our whole reason for coming to Pride in the first place, which is to say I didn't mention it at all, mostly because I didn't know how to tell Dad it was all for him. Part of me hoped that if I just kept talking, Seb would appear and we wouldn't have to admit that we'd lost him. But my mouth was getting dry from all the waffling I was doing to buy us time, and my mind was quickly going blank. By the end of the story, he was nowhere in sight and it looked like I had no choice, but Dad took it out of my hands anyway.

'And where's Seb?' he said carefully, searching the invisible air between me and Bell. 'I know for a fact you don't go anywhere without him. So, where is he?'

Bell accidentally made a noise somewhere between a squawk and a gulp. We were so busted and we both knew it.

'He's . . .' My mouth zipped itself shut of its own accord.

'Any luck yet?' We all whirled around to find Viv and Dora, arm in arm, a shared look of concern between them. 'No sign at the station. We let some of the staff know but nobody's seen sight nor sound of h—'

'HI, VIV!' Oscar spluttered, loud enough to make us all jump. He blushed and looked at the rest of us for help.

'Dad, this is Viv,' I said quietly, unsure how I was going to explain this away. I didn't want to lie, I just needed more time.

'And who, exactly, is Viv,' Dad said in a measured tone.

'Ah, you must be this little one's dad,' Viv said, unhooking her arm from Dora's and reaching out to shake Dad's hand. 'I'm Vivian. This is Dora. We met your son earlier today. I assure you we're doing everything we can to fin—'

Bell coughed pointedly but Viv didn't seem to get the memo and charged on anyway. 'We'll find him, I'm sure. He can't be far away, right?'

All colour immediately drained from Dad's face. 'What do you mean you'll "*find*" him? Where is he?' Dad eyed me again. This time, he looked furiously faint, as if he couldn't quite decide whether to erupt in anger or sit down and hold his head between his knees.

'Did we miss the party?' Lara sang, suddenly appearing from behind a column with Lita and Yan on her tail. Dad sighed weakly, looking at the twins and their purple hair with suspicion.

'Nope, you arrived right on time,' Oscar said, trying to smile with his teeth but giving more of a wince instead.

'Any sign of the kid?' Yan asked softly, rolling his shoulders and stretching his arms. 'We didn't have any luck.'

'Where are the others? And who's this?' Lita looked Dad up and down, but there was no time for introductions.

'A drag queen on time, now there's a horror story if ever I've heard one. Any luck?' Buttercup, possibly even taller than before, strode towards us, Boo bouncing like a spring next to him.

'Not a sight nor sound,' Lara said back, jutting her bottom lip out and looking sad about the whole situation.

'We heard some news!' Boo said, skipping on the spot for something to do. Their face lit up like they were ready to tell us next week's winning lottery numbers. 'People have seen him! He's around here somewhere! We asked some friends and they swore blind they'd seen him not far from here!'

Buttercup shushed Boo swiftly, and they clamped their lips together with what looked like extreme effort. 'It's true,' Buttercup confirmed with a single nod. 'We showed them the picture and they said they'd seen him. And he wasn't alone either! Apparently, he was with a bunch of people who were all wearing yellow, which *really* narrows the search down.' To make his point, a cluster of yellow T-shirt-wearers galloped on by, a lost-looking Seb nowhere in sight.

'What's this about a bunch of people wearing yellow?' Lester joined the circle, Michael hot on his heels. By now, Dad looked exhausted by the sudden arrivals. He blew out his cheeks, clasping his hands tightly together.

'Apparently some people saw Seb earlier, with a group of people wearing yellow.' Viv shrugged like it didn't really mean anything, but Dora suddenly yelped and tugged on her arm.

'Wearing something yellow like, I don't know, fluorescent yellow T-shirts?' Dora pointed wildly behind us, back towards the parade.

We all followed her finger, taking in the crowd, which seemed to have somehow grown again. Sure enough, there was a sunshine-yellow top. And another one. And another. Dozens of them dotted around the crowd suddenly jumped out, flashing suns that held promise and just a glimmer of hope.

'The stewards!' Dora explained, rocking on her heels enough to get Boo excited all over again. 'The volunteers! They're all wearing bright yellow T-shirts!'

'But there's hundreds of them all over the city,' Michael sighed, far from excited about the breakthrough. 'We'll never find him if we're just searching for people wearing yellow.'

Yan raised his hand and shrugged. 'Don't the stewards have little checkpoints? Like, places they can go to take a break or sign off or whatever?' He nudged Lita and Lara,

who nodded. 'We volunteered last year, I'm sure of it.'

Dad, who until now had just been watching this sudden chaos unfold with confusion, intrigue and complete horror, stepped forward into the circle. 'And where's the closest checkpoint? Maybe the stewards have taken Seb there, away from the crowds.'

Yan, Lara and Lita huddled together, silently communicating in search of the answer. It didn't take long for the light bulb to turn on. 'The end of the parade!' Lita shrieked. 'Of course!'

'What are we waiting for then?' Boo said, breathless with adrenaline. 'Let's go!'

Lita and Lara led the way at speed, almost vaulting over each other in their haste. Boo hot-footed it after them, followed by Yan, Michael, Lester, Viv, Dora, Oscar, Dean and Bell. Buttercup tottered along at the back, complaining about poor shoe choices for running in.

Before we could take off after them, Dad pulled me back. He watched as the others rounded the corner, mulling something over in his head. I looked up at him uncertainly, hoping the hammer wasn't about to fall.

'I've missed you, champ,' he said. I couldn't be sure, but I thought I saw the ghost of a smile flit across his face. For a brief moment, I dared to hope.

So, I took the plunge, hoping now was as good a time as any. 'Am I still in trouble?'

'Oh, *big* trouble,' he said. 'But we'll cross that bridge later. First, let's go and find Seb.' And, with a seed of dread blooming in the dungeons of my stomach, we set off after the others.

CHAPTER 32

THE END OF THE RAINBOW

The end of the parade route was all of a hundred metres from where we'd been standing this whole time, just around the corner from the Admiralty Arch. We dived and ducked and dodged our way around people, who were all too happy and full of elation to care about our panicked sprinting. Even when Boo went tumbling into a group of men, clad all in black and with matching beards, managing to spill every drink in the circle, they just raised their empty cups in a jubilant cheer.

This was our last chance to save the day from complete and utter ruin. The clock was ticking ominously over us, counting down towards disaster. *If Seb isn't there* ... I couldn't even bring myself to finish the thought. He *had* to be.

Fighting through the hordes of people was tough work, but eventually we spotted an incredible arch of multicoloured balloons, shaped into a giant rainbow that spread from one side of the road to the other, signalling the end of the parade route. Floats passed under it, met with cheers and screams of elation from the watching crowd. One such float was slowly pulling up beside us, the people aboard hugging each other and still dancing to the music.

'Over there!' Lester yelled over his shoulder, pointing at a huddle of yellow T-shirts a little way past the rainbow arch. Boo and Yan vaulted the barricade and began hurtling off towards them, while Lita gave Lara a boost over the fence. The rest of us were sensible enough to find a gap instead of trying to participate in that game of high jump, legging it through the multicoloured balloons with our fingers and toes crossed for luck. The crowd cheered once more as we hurtled under the arch, as if we'd run a marathon and won.

'What's all this?' said one of the yellow T-shirt wearers as we all screeched to a halt and began jabbering over each other in our haste to explain what was going on.

We must have looked an extraordinary bunch, some of us in make-up, some of us in dresses, some of us with hair that looked like it had been made from threads woven by pixies and fairies. The man blinked as he took us all in. His face really was a picture, his mouth slightly agape so that he looked somewhat dumbfounded.

'How about we try this one at a time?' Dad hollered over everyone else. He whistled harshly, piercing through the chatter, which stopped immediately. 'We're looking for someone. He's been lost for a while now and someone said they saw him with people wearing yellow T-shirts.'

The man looked down at his top, inspecting the colour as if he hadn't put it on himself and had only just realized he was wearing one at all. 'Uhhh, what does he look like?'

Bell marched forward and flipped her phone around. Instinctively, we all leaned closer, waiting for the good news. The man squinted, wrinkling his nose in thought. He looked blank and flat out of options. For something to do, he vaguely flipped open a lid and peered inside a small box labelled 'lost property', like Seb could be hiding at the bottom under all of the sweatshirts and glitter. When he finally looked up, he still appeared baffled.

'Nope, haven't seen him. Sorry,' he added quickly, watching us all visibly deflate. 'I can keep an eye out for him and pass the word around?'

We all nodded half-heartedly. Oscar rested his head on Dean's shoulder, half a second away from bursting into tears. Dean didn't look much better. Neither did Bell or Dad or anybody else. My jaw tightened, as if to stop myself from letting out the cry buried in my throat. This was our last hope and it had just been snuffed out, a candle flame taking on a stormy wind.

'We have to call the police. It's hopeless trying to find him here. Somebody should've called the police when Seb first went missing,' Dad said in a clipped voice, glaring at me, Oscar and Dean. I shrank back, staring at my shoelaces in shame.

'I should call Seb's mum as well, let her know what's happening,' he carried on. 'What a fun conversation that's going to be!' Dad wiped his brow and pulled out his phone, stepping away from us for some space.

'Hi, Sabine, it's Kev,' Dad said after three rings. I could hear the worry in Sabine's voice already. Dad cringed, gritting his teeth. 'I've got something to tell you, but I don't want you to worry, okay? Everything's going to be fine.' He sighed heavily, getting ready to drop the bomb.

But it never came. There was the hum of another Pride float arriving, cheers washing down on us in waves as it went under the balloons. I chanced a glance up at Dad, but he wasn't looking at any one of us. Instead, his eyes were flitting over the float. They settled on something and, because this day couldn't get any weirder, his face split in half with a grin.

'Sabine, I'm gonna call you right back,' he said in a rush, and hung up the phone.

'Wait, is that . . .' Dean said, frowning at the same spot that Dad was transfixed on. I followed his gaze.

The float was slowly moving towards us, dozens of people dressed in exaggerated feathers in every colour on board and still dancing. Some were blowing whistles and setting off party poppers, celebrating the end of the parade. One woman whipped out a long tube, shrieking with laughter as she twisted it in her hands. The tube exploded like a shotgun, enough confetti to cover the road from here to home raining down on everybody.

And there, in the middle of all the balloons and feathers and confetti, peeping over the rails of the float with an uneasy look that I'd recognize anywhere, was my best friend.

'SEB!' Me, Bell, Oscar, Dean and Dad shrieked in unison. We all pelted towards the float, scrambling over each other in our haste to get to him first. Naturally, I got there last, but that's beside the point.

Bell jumped up onto the float first, having bolted out of the blocks at full speed. She leaped onto Seb with enough force to knock over one of the statues in Trafalgar Square. She squealed and shrilled, both pushing him away to get a better look and pulling him in for the tightest hug on record. There was confetti stuck to his head, which still had faint traces of glitter from the train ride, so he looked almost bird-like. But even though his hair covered most of his face, there was no mistaking the look of relief and the slightly wobbly smile that I'd been missing all day.

'You found me,' he breathed, his voice shaking a little. 'I've been looking for you everywhere.' He shook his head, either in wonder or disbelief or just in an attempt to clear it of confetti. His eyes went wide as he noticed the rest of our army, who were in various stages of clambering aboard the float, Buttercup complaining that his dress wasn't made for such activities.

'Where have you been?!' Oscar said, barging through the crowd of feathers and lifting Seb up into the air. 'I never thought I'd be so happy to see your little face in my whole life. I'm not a complete failure at babysitting after all!'

'I wouldn't go that far,' Bell chipped in, still holding onto Seb's sleeve.

'Hey, man, glad you could make the party after all,' Dean said, ruffling loose the last remaining confetti feathers from Seb's head. 'What took you so long?'

Oscar put Seb back down on his feet and the two of us locked eyes. I didn't waste any time trying to say something smart or clever or witty. I'm not sure I'd have been able to. Instead, I ducked under Dean's elbow and crashed into Seb, wrapping my arms around him. I was almost scared to let go in case we lost him all over again. In case, like a balloon, he'd be lifted up and away by the breeze if I didn't hold on tight.

When we finally broke apart, it looked like he was about to say something. But his face suddenly fell, drooping in horror like melted candle wax as he spotted Dad standing at the back of the float, his arms crossed across his chest. He looked kind of mad but also relieved, both emotions playing a tug-of-war across his face. Seb might've really fainted this time if I hadn't been holding onto his elbow.

'It's okay,' I said quietly out of the side of my mouth, trying not to move my lips

314

so Dad wouldn't see. 'I explained it wasn't your fault.' My words of comfort didn't have the desired effect, and Seb only seemed to wind himself tighter under Dad's watch.

'Where've you *been*?!' Bell nearly shrieked, grabbing Seb by the shoulders and fit to burst with the questions we'd all been thinking. 'How did we even lose you in the first place?! You were right there and then suddenly you weren't! And why didn't you come straight to the arch?!' She was speaking so quickly that her words were squashed together into one long sound.

Seb looked nervously around at us all, his mouth twitching like it didn't know whether to grimace or smile. He glanced at Dad, who gave him a half-nod which seemed to breathe some air into his lungs.

'I don't think you'd believe me, even if I told you,' he said.

CHAPTER 33

THE END, KINDA

We listened to Seb's story there on the float, oohing and aahing with wonder (and maybe a little apprehension, even though we all knew how the tale ended). It turned out that Seb hadn't been alone for long, having quite literally stumbled into the middle of the dancers and their feathers. The dancers who were still on the float cheered at that part, which made Seb glow with a knowing and mischievous grin.

'Ah, you must be the friends we've been searching high and low for.' A woman hopped up onto the float, her purple feathers stretching up towards the sky. Her hair was pinned to the top of her head in an elegant shape, crowned with flowers.

'I'm Clara,' she beamed warmly, gesturing to the other dancers. 'And this is our little Pride family. We're called Kaleidoscope.' Another cheer bubbled from the feathers around us. Clara giggled, a melodic sound that made me want to laugh too. 'This little one's been looking for you everywhere. But he's been safe and sound with us in the parade. I think we've even found our newest member of the Kaleidoscope gang. You've got some rhythm, kid!'

Me and Bell gawped at that, our jaws hitting the floor. Seb blushed as Clara gave him a quick hug, her purple feathers ruffling as she laughed. Her infectious energy was enough to soften Dad a little, which is to say that he no longer looked like he was about to explode or burst into tears. I guess that was all we could ask for considering we'd been caught red-handed.

He stepped forward and shook Clara's hand, thanking her endlessly for bringing Seb back to us safe and sound. Oscar and Dean also thanked Clara profusely, clearly relieved to have had their backsides saved.

'No worries at all,' she said brightly. 'I'm glad to get the family back together again. You enjoy the rest of your Pride now! And hey, try not to get lost again, okay? You can't dance with Kaleidoscope next year if we can't find you!'

High-fiving Seb, Clara gave us all an air kiss and hopped off the float after the other purple feathers, who were retreating down the road with a bounce in their step. That just left our little group of colourful warriors on board.

'All's well that ends well, then!' Lester said, taking us all in. 'Everybody back together and accounted for?' Dad swept his eyes across us all and nodded to himself. 'Well, in that case, I hate to rush but we really do have a show to be getting on with.'

Lester looked at himself in his pocket mirror and gasped so loud that I thought he might accidentally cough up his lungs. 'Hideous!' he wheezed. 'I can't believe you've let me walk around looking like *this*!' He quickly began patting at his face, Boo bobbing up and down on the spot and watching avidly.

'Let's get this ball rolling then,' Buttercup said grandly. 'Five minutes to get your wigs and lipstick on, ladies! Our stage awaits!'

A pang of sadness washed over me as our group hopped off the float and dived into action, flinging open bags and suitcases, a hurricane of wigs and lipsticks flying all around. This was it. Our day was to end here. I glanced

at Dad, certain that we were about to be sent home with immediate effect and a lifetime grounding. Bell and Seb hovered next to me, fidgeting with guilt now that everything had calmed down.

'Can I talk to you guys for a second?' Dad said. But he wasn't talking to us – he nodded in the direction of Oscar and Dean, who were looking like the Holy Ghost had passed before their eyes. They gulped and stepped aside with Dad.

'What do you think they're talking about?' Bell said uncertainly, watching as the three of them huddled and began talking intently.

'It's obvious, isn't it? He's deciding our fates! How many summers to ground us for! Which of our parents to tell first!' Seb's entire body trembled and shuddered. Mine did too, for that matter.

'Well, in my books, when you get caught, you need to make a miraculous escape to avoid prison or, in our case, a lifetime grounding.' Bell narrowed her eyes, thinking hard. 'Does anybody have a trench coat?'

When the conversation was done, Oscar and Dean stepped away, heads bowed like disgraced schoolkids. 'He wants to talk to you,' Oscar mumbled in my general direction, not looking up. I glanced over at Dad, who had clasped his hands together in an 'I really mean business' kind of way.

'Good luck!' Bell and Seb whispered as I slouched over to where my fate surely stood.

I didn't dare look up for fear of what I might see. You know when your parents say they're not mad, they're just *disappointed*, and somehow you wish they'd just be cross instead? I didn't want to see the disappointment written on Dad's face. I didn't want the space between us, that I'd been trying so desperately to fix, to just get even wider.

'I don't need to tell you that you're in big trouble, right?' Dad began. I shook my head, still staring at my shoelaces. 'What were you thinking, coming all the way here? You not only broke a million rules to do so, but you brought Bell and Seb along too and put everyone in danger. What if we had never found Seb? What if something bad had happened? An accident and someone got hurt because we weren't here to protect you?' Dad's voice quivered, his eyes suspiciously watery.

'I didn't mean to,' I mumbled. It sounded feeble and pathetic, but I carried on anyway. 'I didn't think things would go this badly. I just thought if ... if we could come for the day and ...' I let the small breeze snatch the rest of the sentence away.

'But why would you need to come here at all?'

'Because . . .' I faltered. 'Because I didn't want things to change, and Oscar said they wouldn't but they did and I just wanted everything to go back to how it was when everybody was happy.'

'But why would coming here change that?'

I didn't know how to say it with words, so I unzipped my bag and found the only explanation I could give – the picture of me and Dad, 'Victor & Junior' scrawled on the back. It was a little wrinkled now, but our smiles were somehow even brighter than I remembered them.

'I wanted us to be like them again,' I said, pointing at the photo. 'I just wanted everything to be like it was before.'

Dad took the picture carefully and studied it for a second. He half-smiled to himself and reached into his pocket for his wallet. He flipped it over and turned it round so I could see. There, smiling back at me, was the same picture – the two of us sitting in the diner at Mack's Arcade with milkshakes and chips between us.

'This was us, and it still is,' Dad said. His voice was low and sincere, quietly fierce with a glimmer of pride hiding underneath. 'We'll never lose that, I promise. This photo,

it comes with me everywhere I go. I might not be with you every day, but you're always with me.' He pulled me into a bear hug, like the ones I'd been missing. The ones only Dad could give. The sounds of Pride swirled around us like a blessing.

'You all right?' Dad said. I nodded, and it wasn't a lie. With Dad's arms around me, I felt safe and like everything just might be okay after all.

'I don't know how to say this,' he continued quietly. 'Before I told you, I imagined what I'd say and how I'd say it and how you'd react and how I'd react and how everything would just figure itself out. I had it all mapped out in my head. I knew things would be a little awkward to begin with and that it might take a bit of work. But I've done this all wrong. I can see that now.'

Dad sighed to himself. 'I've been burying my head in the sand for the longest time. I guess I was just hoping that when I pulled it back out, everything would be fine and we could go on as normal. This should've been so easy to put right.'

Dad pulled me into another one-armed hug and rested his head on mine. 'I'm sorry, Archie. For tipping your world upside down and then not being there to help you put things right again.'

'You don't need to be sorry, you haven't done anything wrong.' I mumbled into his jacket. 'But I'm sorry. For, you know, coming here and making you worry.'

'I was gonna ask you to come here with me, you know?' Dad chuckled to himself. 'I didn't think you'd want to and I guess I chickened out. That'll teach me for keeping things to myself.'

Dad looked at me thoughtfully. 'Promise me I won't have to go alone next time?' He gestured at Pride around us, pointing back up to the parade and beyond.

I couldn't fight the grin spreading across my face. 'I promise,' I said.

By now, everyone was in various states of disarray, and I watched as my friends, both old and new, put the finishing touches to their looks. Viv and Dora sat together, holding hands and glancing over at us every now and then. Boo was all but jogging on the spot, ready to go. Lester and Michael had finally put their wigs and eyebrows on and were now furiously dabbing lipsticks as if they were lightsabres ready for war. Buttercup was struggling to stop himself from hurrying everybody along and was doing an awful job at hiding it. Lara and Lita were braiding Yan's hair into intricate plaits – he looked so relaxed that on first glance it would've been fair to assume he was fast asleep in Lara's lap. Bell and Seb were huddled together with Oscar and Dean, trying not to make it obvious that they were doing everything in their power to listen in.

As I took it all in, the sparks of joy suddenly fizzled, replaced by a whirl of gloom. Now, our adventure was really over.

'I guess we're going home then,' I said, trying not to let my disappointment show but not exactly doing a great job.

'What? And miss this show everyone's been talking about? Think again, mister.' Dad grinned and gave my shoulder a squeeze. 'Let's go and see what all the fuss is about, and then we'll think about getting us all home in one piece.'

In my daze, I didn't understand what I'd just heard. Surely, I'd replaced what Dad had said with the words I actually wanted to hear. But then a sudden surge, a tremble of adrenaline, jolted through me.

'We can stay?'

Dad didn't even have time to finish his nod before I jumped up in the air, throwing my arms around his neck. The adventure wasn't over yet! And now we could carry it on without breaking any rules or getting into any trouble, and hopefully nobody getting lost for good measure.

'Finally!' Buttercup said as we rejoined the group. 'Let's get a shimmy on, our spotlights won't wait for ever you know!'

We made a start, falling into a loose huddle as we ambled towards this stage that everybody had been speaking of. Dad was in as good a mood as anybody else, which got me thinking about something important.

'Dad?' I said carefully.

'Mmm?'

I took a deep breath. 'Am I grounded?'

Dad looked at his phone, where thirty-two missed calls from Sabine glared back at him. 'Most definitely,' he said. 'But ten points for trying.'

CHAPTER 34

EVERYTHING WILL BE ALBRIGHT

So, that was last summer. The whole story from start to finish. I got grounded for two weeks because, even though Dad forgave me and swore to high heaven that he wasn't mad, he still said that actions have consequences. Apparently taking responsibility for things is part and parcel of being an adult, which sounds gross to me but I guess it makes sense. I argued that *technically* I wasn't yet an adult so surely this didn't apply to me. Dad saw the funny side, even though I was being deadly serious, and brought my sentence down to a week, with no PlayStation. I grumbled and groaned, but it was the best outcome I could've asked for.

As for Mum, she was more worried than anything and

made me promise that I would never do anything that stupid ever again. Considering the day that we'd had, it was hardly a chore to take that oath. After Dad dropped me off at the house, he spoke to Mum in the kitchen for hours. Like, literally hours, I'm not even kidding. It was almost midnight when he came upstairs to say goodbye, but Mum followed him up and suggested that he stay the night instead. We blew up the air bed and he slept right beside my bed, the way Seb and Bell do when they sleep over. The only difference is their snoring doesn't keep me up for half the night.

Sure, Mum and Dad still have their *moments*. That's what I call it when they're having a disagreement. Dad says it's because they both love me so much. Mum says it's because she loves me more, which makes Dad laugh. They're kind of friends now, I suppose. Whatever was said between them in the kitchen after we got home from Pride has definitely smoothed things over. Now they just bicker, but it never ends in tears so that, my friends, is what we call progress.

In the spirit of never doing anything as stupid as last year, this summer was completely different. For one, I'm now thirteen and a teenager and definitely more of an adult than I was twelve months ago. I'm sure if I got lost in the middle of London again, I could solve the problem, no worries at all. But this year, I didn't have to. Why, I hear you ask? Because this year, we had company.

'Up and at 'em, folks!' Dad's cheery voice jolted me from my sleep. The sun was already beaming from behind my curtains, birds tweeting their morning (and rather irritating) song.

'What time is it?' I moaned, pulling a pillow over my head.

'Time to get your butt up and out of that bed, mister,' said Dad, hitting me with the other pillow for good measure. 'Downstairs in ten, I've got the breakfast on.' Sure enough, the smell of bacon came floating up the stairs on his heels.

'Come on, sweetheart,' Mum said sleepily from the doorway, fighting off a yawn. 'We've got a long day ahead of us and you need some food in you before we get going.'

'Five more minutes,' I grumbled, still half asleep. Mum laughed and flopped onto the bed next to me.

'I'm sure we can trust him in the kitchen for five minutes without burning the house down,' she said. Famous last words – sixty seconds later, the fire alarm went off and roused us all determinedly.

'What's on fire?' Bell yawned from the heap of sheets on the floor.

'The house, most probably, if not half the street by now.' Mum shook the sleep away from her and trotted out of the room to fix whatever mess Dad had created downstairs.

'A guilt-free bacon sandwich this year,' said Seb, his head popping up and following the smell of cooked, if not slightly burnt, food. 'This year's already better than the last.'

Downstairs, Mum had managed to salvage most of the bacon, although some of it sizzled in the bin, black and smoking. She cut the sandwiches in neat halves and placed the plate in the middle of the table. Dad thanked her with a hug and plonked himself down next to me as Seb swallowed half a sandwich in one gulp, barely taking a breath before inhaling the rest.

'Make sure you save some for your parents,' Mum trilled, putting down an extra plate of food for good measure.

On cue, the front door opened and in waltzed Sabine. She planted a big kiss on Seb's cheek and took her spot next to him at the table, leaning over to conspire with Mum about the latest goings on between Mr Quarterman and Mrs Fielder.

Bell's parents weren't far behind, arm in arm as they walked into our kitchen, bear-hugging Bell from both sides. 'All set for the big day?' Geoff said, letting go of Kathy's arm so he could scoop up a bacon sandwich. Baby Jack was at his grandma's for the weekend, which Bell was trying hard not to look *too* happy about.

'You bet!' Dad said between mouthfuls of his own.

With full and content stomachs, we gathered our things for the day and regrouped on the driveway under the basking sun, which was already heating up the day like warm water in a cold bath. The screech of tyres announced the arrival of the final two members of our troop. Oscar jumped out from behind the steering wheel of a rather beat-up car, paint flaking from the dented doors. I've never seen anyone love anything the way Oscar loves that car, which he got after passing his driving test. I think even Dean was taking a back seat to the car, which Oscar had called Linda for good measure.

'Ready to go when you are,' Dean said, looking slightly green after Oscar's driving. His hair was back to brown this year, although if he flicked it up in just the right way, you could see hints of blue underneath.

We all piled into the minibus parked on the kerb

outside my house, Dad taking the keys and jumping into the driving seat. 'Are you sure don't want me to drive?' Oscar tried, already grumbling about having to sit in the back with us regular folk.

'Oscar, you can't be trusted to babysit three kids without losing them,' Dad said under his breath. Mum still didn't know *that* bit of the story. 'You're *definitely* not driving from here to London. I value my life, thank you very much.' Dean looked somewhat relieved at that and relaxed in his seat. Oscar folded his arms and looked grumpily out of the window.

'All ready?' Dad called.

'Yeah!' we all chorused back.

And then we were off. London Pride awaited on the horizon and this year, we were doing it right, with our families by our side. If I learned anything from last year, it's that Pride is all about family, both the ones you're given and the ones you make. Somewhere fifty miles or so away, Lester and Michael and Dora and Viv and the rest of our army would be getting ready for the big day. Clara and Kaleidoscope were no doubt warming up too, much to Seb's delight. They'd all be meeting us in London, so we could do Pride properly – together.

And I guess that's where our story ends. Things always get better if you only give it a little time. You don't need to run off to London to try and fix them. I learned that the hard way so you don't have to.

When I think about it, Dad didn't really change at all. He's still terrible at cooking and even worse at air hockey. He still watches *Top Gun* at least once a month. He still bites his lower lip so his teeth are showing when he's concentrating really hard and he doesn't wear his glasses when he's supposed to. He still loves me and Mum. And he's still my dad too.

As for Mum, she'd kill me if she knew *all* the details of what happened last year. Sabine would probably faint on the spot. But I think I trust you to only give this story to people who can keep a secret. I'll let you be the one to decide that.

I appreciate your co-operation and secrecy, partner.

Until next time,

Your friend, Archie Maverick Albright.

ACKNOWLEDGEMENTS

In what is potentially the most unprofessional way to start book acknowledgements, I just want to say ... I DID IT! Writing a book can be such a solitary experience, especially at the beginning when you're not even sure if your book will make it onto a shelf. But, although an author writes the words, it's a team project and there are a million people I have to thank in only a handful of words. I'm sorry but you're all only getting first names – you know who you are!

First to Alice, who fell out of the sky like an actual angel. Thank you for gently pushing me in the direction of children's books – you really did know best!

Also, to my agent Chloe, who helped steer the ship

home and indulged more emails about Little Mix/ replacing the Mona Lisa with my book cover than actual work.

Archie and his rainbow army wouldn't have a home if it wasn't for the wonders at Simon & Schuster. I'm incredibly lucky to have landed a dream publisher and it's all thanks to my endlessly talented editor, Lucy. I hope you're proud of what we did!

And to Melissa, Ali, Eve, Daniel, Rachel, Laura and the entire team who worked on this – I can't ever thank you enough. You've made my dreams come true.

Also, the biggest thank you to my illustrator, Sandhya Prabhat, for bringing my story to life with such vibrancy and colour. You are truly a magician.

I wouldn't have been able to type a single word if it wasn't for the love and support of my best friends. Ellen, by my side for 15 years and counting (you're never getting rid of me, even when you're on the other side of the world); Matthew, my partner in (*Fortnite*) crime and all-around angel; Jack, the Geri to my Victoria always and forever; Ellie, my best colleague who I never talk to past 5pm because we're only work friends; and Gena, who hasn't managed to replace me (yet).

Also, to my Ladies Who Lunch squad and my Goslings clique – you're all absolute diamonds and I love you more than words. And a special shout out to Tessington for all the pep talks and coffee breaks, and to Ellie W for just about everything over the last three years.

To my little sister, Ellie, here's your name in a book. I hope this gives me cool big brother points. And Gran, Sammy Ferguson's all grown up now! I hope you're proud.

Finally, Mum. I know you're probably already crying – they better be happy tears! I'll never be able to thank you for everything you've done for me. I love you times infinity plus one. This book is for you.

BENJAMIN DEAN

© Laura Gallant

Benjamin Dean is a London-based celebrity reporter. His biggest achievement to date is breaking the news that Rihanna can't wink (she blinks, in case you were wondering). Benjamin can be found on Twitter as @notagainben tweeting about Rihanna and LGBTQ+ culture to his 10,000+ followers. *Me, My Dad and the End of the Rainbow* is his debut book and he's currently working on his second, publishing in 2022.

SANDHYA PRABHAT

Sandhya Prabhat is an illustrator and animator originally from Chennai, India and currently living in California. She loves illustrating children's books, animated stickers and videos for social media platforms, and for TV and movies. Her work can be seen at www.sandhyaprabhat.com and she can be followed on Instagram @sandhyaprabhat

ME, MY DAD AND THE END OF THE RAINBOW

is also available to listen to as an audiobook!

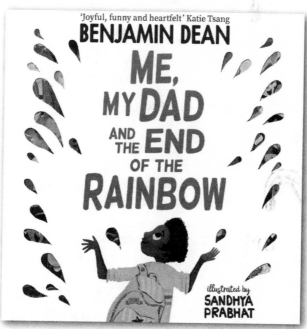

'Joyful, funny and heartfelt' Katie Tsang

BENJAMIN DEAN

ME, MY DAD AND THE END OF THE RAINBOW

illustrated by
SANDHYA PRABHAT

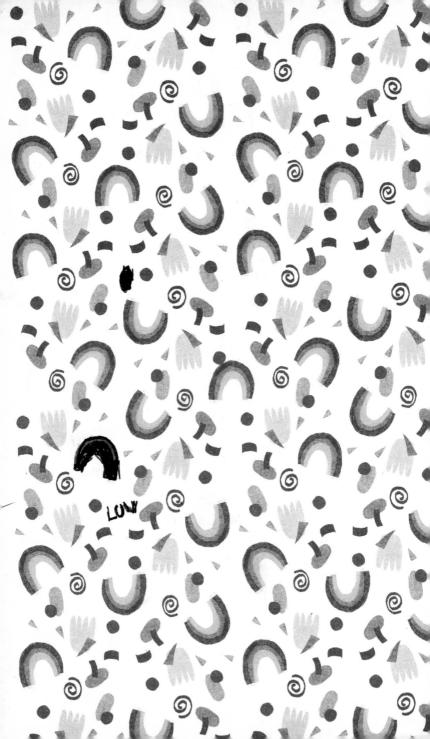